UNDERCOVER GIRL

by

NIGEL HUMPHREY

DORRANCE PUBLISHING CO., INC.
PITTSBURGH, PENNSYLVANIA 15222

All Rights Reserved
Copyright © 2003 by Nigel Humphrey
No part of this book may be reproduced or transmitted
in any form or by any means, electronic or mechanical,
including photocopying, recording, or by any information
storage and retrieval system without permission in writing
fromm the publisher

ISBN # 0-8059-5903-3
Printed in the United States of America

First Printing

For information or to order additional books, please write:
Dorrance Publishing Co., Inc.
701 Smithfield Street
Third Floor
Pittsburgh, Pennsylvania 15222
U.S.A.
1-800-788-7654
Or visit our web site and on-line catalog at *www.dorrancepublishing.com*

I dedicate this book to April Humphrey, Stephanie May, Misty Crawford, Pastor Valerie Jones and family, and to Rodney Weekly and his family.

CONTENTS

Chapter 1 Mickey 1

Chapter 2 Wheels of Justice 6

Chapter 3 The Killer 11

Chapter 4 On the Trail 15

Chapter 5 Shakedown 19

Chapter 6 A Bigger Piece of the Puzzle 28

Chapter 7 The Enigma 35

Chapter 8 Hook, Line, and Sinker 40

Chapter 9 Deadly Game 45

Chapter 10 The Message 51

Chapter 11 The Feds 58

Chapter 12 First Strike 63

Chapter 13 Assault 67

Chapter 14 A Hand Up 73

Chapter 15 Infiltration 76

Chapter 16 Case Closed 80

ACKNOWLEDGEMENTS

First I want to thank Jesus Christ, my Lord and Savior, for instilling this talent in me, My wife, April, for her love, support, and computer skills. My grandfather, J.C. Staples, and my sister, Stephanie Marie May, for always believing in me, Bailey Williams and the Williams family, Bishop Michael A. Bates and the New Birth Church Family for their encouragement, La Troy McDaniel for some suggestions for the book, and Pastor Rufus Connor and Conner family. Very importantly, Dr. John Johnson, for all his help, information, encouragement and expertise in getting this book off the ground. I'd like to also acknowledge my creative writing teacher Lisa Koger for her inspiration and encouragement.

INTRODUCTION

Every day we hear news about the high crime rate in cities across the United States. During the time period between the 80's and the year 2000, the crime rate has risen dramatically. This story, set some time in the 1980's depicts a young detective's struggle against crime in the city of Santa Bella, California, proving that once the wheels of justice start turning, nothing can stop them.

CHAPTER 1

MICKEY

Lieutenant Cassi Day walked briskly through the hospital Corridors, occasionally twisting and dodging to avoid bumping into the bustling personnel.

She felt sick. It had been only four days since her partner was shot and as she hurried to find his room, she couldn't shake the overwhelming feeling of dread that had gripped her entrails like an invisible hand, twisting them into a knot.

As she boarded an elevator she silently prayed that Mick would be conscious, but was unsure of what to say to him if he was.

The elevator stopped several times, admitting new passengers, and each stop made Cassi more and more impatient. She felt anger rising within her and did her best to suppress it.

When it seemed like she was going to explode, the elevator finally came to the seventeenth floor. When the doors opened Cassi strode out so quickly that she nearly ran over an orderly who was passing by.

"Whoa," he said, looking lustfully at the attractive young woman. "Where's the fire, babe?"

Having dealt with his kind before, Cassi turned on him, unclipped her badge from her belt and held it up for him to see. "I'm not your babe or anybody's. I'm a cop!"

Clearly shaken, the man backed away under her glare. "I'm sorry officer," he stammered "I... I didn't know."

Cassi glared at him a moment longer then resumed her quick pace, slowly regaining her composure. She kept walking until she reached the duty nurse's desk.

"Yes, may I help you?" said the nurse.

"Yeah, I'm looking for Mick Colton's room."

The nurse looked in her patient book and found Mick's room number. "Here it is, room 1722. Go down the hall, hang a left, and its two doors down."

"Thanks," said Cassi.

As she turned to leave, the nurse spoke again. "Excuse me, are you Cassi?"

"Yeah, that's me." She answered.

"Good. He was asking for you earlier today."

Cassi's spirits rose and her eyes glowed with the news. Mick was conscious...or at least had been, which kept her hope alive. "Thanks again". She said. Following the nurse's directions, Cassi was soon approaching Mick's room. With her heart pounding, she stopped Just outside the door, trying to calm herself. She then took a deep breath and walked through the door.

Mick lay still. His eyes were closed but he was breathing regularly. His ebony skin was glistening with sweat as his muscular chest rose and fell with each breath. The EKG monitor's soft beeping was the only sound in the room, and the sight of her friend hooked up to it made her sicker than she was already. But she forced herself to look anyway.

As an undercover cop, Cassi had seen several innocents caught and shot up in deadly gunfights on the streets. And too often officers, many of whom she knew, had stopped bullets, never to rise again. She knew the score, as every good cop did. "When you play in the street, its part of the game." But this time it was different. Now it was her partner lying there with his life hanging in the balance. She could accept the way things turned out, but that didn't mean she had to like it.

Swallowing a lump in her throat, Cassi looked around and picked up a chair and set it close to Mick's bed. It wasn't until she sat down that she realized how tired she was. Since the warehouse raid, she'd been filing reports, interrogating suspects, checking ballistic reports on bullets recovered after the fighting, and following up on clues and information obtained from suspects. The raid had been highly successful, but costly. Many officers, including Mick, were shot.

Wearily she leaned forward. "Mickey, I don't know if you can hear me but... It's Cassi. I'm here now, partner."

Mick hadn't moved. His eyes were still closed, but now his breathing sounded labored. But at least he was still breathing. She leaned back, propped an elbow on the chair's armrest, and covered her face with one hand. Tears rolled down her cheeks as she softly whispered, "Blast you, Mick Colton. You die on me, I'll kill' ya." Cassi then closed her eyes and within minutes fell into exhausted sleep.

Hours later she awoke with a start, looking around frantically. When she saw the EKG monitor was still beeping she relaxed, relieved that Mick was still among the living. Cassi rubbed her eyes and checked her watch. It was 5:30 a.m. *Jeez, I've been out cold eight hours!* she thought.

She rose wearily to her feet and stretched, feeling her back pop as she did. It felt good to relieve the tension of the last four days. She pushed her chair back and was about to go to the lounge for a cup of coffee when Mick stirred. "C- Cassi?"

She whirled around, startled and overjoyed. "Mickey"? His eyes were open to mere slits, but he could see his partner's angelic features clearly as she walked over and knelt beside him.

"Cassi," He repeated, weakly.

"Yeah, Mickey," She said, holding one of his hands. "I'm here."

"I... I guess I... can't look out for you anymore, honey."

" Don't say that, Mickey," Cassi said. "The doc'll fix you up and you'll be back on the street in no time."

"Only God can...can perform miracles," Mick stuttered. "It's my fault.... too careless."

"No, no!" Cassi said, urgently. "You saved my life."

"I...I love ya' kid." Mick said. His breathing slowed more and more then stopped all together and his hand went limp and slipped out of Cassi's. The EKG's beeping was now replaced by a long high-pitched moan, signaling the end of Mick Colton's life.

"Mick?" Tears of anger and grief flowed down Cassi's cheeks as she stared at her fallen partner. "Oh God... M-Mick!" She stood and backed slowly away from the bed as the nurses, having heard the monitor, came rushing into the room. In helpless rage, Cassi Day slammed her fist against the wall, startling the nurses. "N-no!" She screamed. Unable to stand the sight of her dead friend any longer, she turned and bolted out of the room and down the hall.

When she reached the ground floor, Cassi ran out of the elevator, through the hallway, and out the double-doors and jumped into her Trans AM. Jerking the car into gear, she floored the accelerator and roared out of the parking lot, leaving skid marks on the pavement. She drove for hours, angrily brushing tears from her eyes and pounding her fist on the dashboard, thinking every minute of the friend she'd left at the hospital and all the years they'd spent together. During good times and bad, each had been there for the other. Now a bullet had taken away everything. No more would she hear Mick laugh or crack a joke. No more would he cover her in a gunfight or listen to her when she needed a friend. There was no more anything now, except emptiness.

When Cassi reached the beach, she pulled the car over, got out, and ran across the sand toward the water, shrugging out of her jacket. She fell to her knees in the shallow surf and with tears still streaming down her face, flung her head back and screamed up to the heavens, "Mickeeeeeey!"

The wind and the waves were the only answer to her mournful cry.

In Los Angeles, two men drove along one of the many highways leading to the down town area. Nick Freeman, kept his eyes locked on the street ahead of them while the passenger, Jack Rhodes, stared nervously at the passing scenery, Silently dreading his destination.

Rhodes, also known as Fresno Jack, was a small time hustler, who'd pulled a few capers out in Fresno, California. He wanted to be a big shot, but the Syndicate he worked for only used him as a delivery and pick-up boy. If he could just get Freeman out of the way then he'd be the boss' right hand man. He didn't know how he'd do it, but things had a way of happening.

Freeman, known as Rock, had been a bare-knuckle fighter in the South Bronx area of New York. He later joined the service and spent three years as a member of the elite Marine Force Recon. During his fourth year he was dishonorably discharged for striking two officers, and an NCO. He wandered the streets with little purpose for two years before the Syndicate took him in. He knew that Rhodes was thinking of taking him on, but wasn't worried. Rhodes didn't have the guts to cross him and if he tried, he'd be taking a dirt nap. Freeman would see to it.

Rhode's arm throbbed due to a gunshot wound he'd gotten in the warehouse raid, luckily for him the bullet had gone in and out, missing the bone, otherwise his left arm would've been shattered. But that was the least of his worries. He had no idea how to tell his boss he'd lost a five million dollar Cocaine shipment in the raid. Would the boss kill him on the spot, or would he bide his time and toy with him? Fresno Jack had no way of knowing, but he did know that no one disappointed Scorpio and lived to tell of it.

"The boss is gonna have a field day with this."

The comment startled Rhodes out of his daydreaming. "What?"

"I said the boss is gonna have a field day with this."

"Just drive the car, will ya'?"

Freeman Chuckled ruefully and shook his head as the car spiraled down a ramp, went under an overpass and into the downtown traffic. The men drove north for six blocks then turned west, heading straight for the dark gray skyscraper that was the Techno Computer Company. The sun was just peeking over the horizon behind them as they stopped at the guard station. The security officer reached down from the window and took the men's ID cards. After a quick inspection he returned their cards, raised the control arm, and waved them through. Freeman pulled the car into one of the reserved spaces nearest the building and killed the engine.

"Show Time." he said, grinning wickedly at Rhodes, who rolled his eyes and got out of the car.

The man known as Scorpio sat with his back to his desk, looking out the glass window at the city below him. His snowy, white hair and frigid voice, combined with the way he dealt with his enemies, had earned him the chilling nickname, "The Ice Man." He thought of Los Angeles as his city, where everything he wanted was at his fingertips. He was well educated in business and finance and could make a decent living in either field, but his drug cartels brought in so much more money. No one who worked for him knew his real name and no one dared ask. His discipline was strict and merciless, and no one had ever quit the powerful Syndicate he'd built.

The intercom on his desk buzzed and he swiveled his chair around to answer it. "Yes?" he said, releasing the talk button.

"Freeman and Rhodes to see you, Sir." said the voice on the other end.

"Send them in." Scorpio rested his elbows on his desk and interlaced his fingers as the door opened and the two men came in. Regarding them with cold, blue green eyes, he said, "Gentlemen, make me happy."

Cassi's car pulled into the garage of her Santa Bella home, as the sun cleared the eastern horizon. The young lady who sat behind the wheel was older and grimmer than the one who was at Mick Colton's side the night before. For a few moments she sat staring out her windshield, dazed. Her eyes where red but her tears were gone...she had no more to shed.

Slowly, almost mechanically, she got out of the car and locked it, feeling cold and empty as she walked to her house, as if someone had reached inside and ripped her very soul from her body.

Locking the front door behind her, Cassi strode through the living room, down the hallway, and into her bedroom, where she removed her wet clothes and dropped them into the hamper. Inwardly, she was glad to have a couple of days off so she could rest and get her head together. She didn't know what she'd do during her off time, but she knew she didn't want to see Mick's body again before the funeral. His death had hurt her enough as it was.

Clad in a short, black bathrobe, Cassi drew herself a hot bath, and when the tub was full, removed her robe and eased into the steaming water. She leaned back and closed her eyes. The hot water felt good and relaxed her tight muscles as she lounged in the sparkling suds. Her mind went blank in the calm darkness, and she was unaware of everything except the soothing water.

Cassi relaxed a few minutes longer then lathered up and washed away the dirt and sand from the beach. After her bath she felt a bit better. She dried herself, put on a fresh set of underwear and her robe, and then went into the living room to watch TV. She clicked the television on with her remote then lay down on the couch, looking at the screen but not really seeing or hearing what was going on. Her eyelids got heavier and heavier and she rolled onto her back, looking up at the ceiling. Within minutes, she was asleep.

Scorpio slowly circled the now seated figure of Jack Rhodes, looking for all of the world like a wolf about to attack its prey while Nick Freeman stood leaning on a nearby wall, chewing a stick of gum.

Rhodes was already nervous, but after seeing the cold-steel glare in Scorpio's eyes he was simply terrified.

"You seem to be favoring your arm, Mr. Rhodes," He said calmly, stopping in front of the man. "Did you have an accident by any chance?"

"N- no sir, I got shot at the warehouse."

"I see..." Said Scorpio. His voice was still calm but now had an edge as cold as his eyes. "So am I to understand that the shipment was...confiscated by the police?"

"Y- yes, sir." Rhodes stammered.

Scorpio resumed his slow pacing, this time passing on Rhodes' left. As he did so he drew back his hand and delivered a vicious Judo chop to Rhodes' shoulder, dislocating it. Howling in pain, Fresno Jack Rhodes fell to the floor only to have the syndicate boss jerk him to his feet.

"You incompetent fool!" Scorpio raged, shaking the man's lapels.

"Do you know how much your collective, ego-driven stupidity cost us?"

"P-Please, sir." Rhodes pleaded." It wasn't my fault. I planned everything down to the last detail. It-It was that cop."

Scorpio tightened his grip on the man's jacket and shook him some more "What cop?"

"T-that broad...and her partner, the one who shut down your racket in Burbank."

Scorpio loosened his grip on Rhodes' jacket. "The one called Day? Cassi Day?"

"Y-Yeah, boss. That's her," said Rhodes.

"Rhodes if I find you've lied to me, I'll..."

"Sir, I'd bet my life on it."

Scorpio's eyes bored into Rhodes and the cold edge came back into his voice. "If you're lying...you'll lose it." And with that, he took hold of Rhode's arm and popped his shoulder back into place. Rhodes cried out again, tears collecting in his eyes as he clutched his sore arm. Scorpio walked calmly to his chair and sat down behind his highly polished, oak desk.

"Go home and get some rest, Jack," he said, again interlacing his fingers.

"I'll have another job for you soon."

"S- sure, boss." Rhodes said, turning to leave. He was almost to the door when Scorpio spoke again.

"And Jack, don't disappoint me again."

CHAPTER 2

WHEELS OF JUSTICE

Cassi's heart pounded with excitement as she made her way through the dimly lit corridor. A fierce battle had erupted between the police and some drug runners. All around her people yelled, guns boomed, radios squawked, and sirens wailed. Suddenly, a figure lunged out of the shadows at her, aiming a pistol. "Look out!" Someone yelled, pushing her out of the way.

Cassi fell down as two weapons roared in the night, spitting fire and lead at each other. She looked back and saw Mick Colton lying on the floor, bleeding from a stomach wound.

Enraged, Cassi jumped to her feet and fired her weapon at the assailant, hitting him in the arm. The man dropped his weapon and gave her a pained expression before he turned and ran for a window at the end of the hall.

"Hold it!" Cassi yelled, but the man kept running. She fired again and missed as the attacker dove through the window.

Cassi awoke suddenly, trying to shake the dream away. She propped herself up on her elbows and looked around groggily. Her clock read 1:30 p.m. and a soap opera was on TV. She didn't know which one...she didn't care. Swinging her legs over the side of the couch, Cassi got up and went to the kitchen to make some coffee. While the water heated she changed into clean blue jeans and a black short-sleeved baseball Jersey she'd brought from the bedroom. Dozens of emotions flooded through her, conflicting each other in civil war. Sadness, anger, and guilt were the most intense. As she walked through the living room, she accidentally knocked over a picture on her coffee table. It was a picture of her, Mickey, and his little sister, Tina, at the beach. Smiling, Cassi stood between them with her arms around them, while they both held up two-fingered peace signs and grinned at the camera. She smiled faintly at the memory then replaced the picture.

Cassi poured herself a cup of coffee and was about to take a sip when someone rang her doorbell. She set the cup down, grabbed her 9mm Beretta from the bedroom, and eased cautiously to the front door. She looked through the peek hole and saw Mick's sister, Christina, standing outside. Her entrails went numb, and she swallowed a choking lump that had come into her throat. This was the moment she'd dreaded. Cassi didn't know how Christina would handle the news about Mick, but she knew she had to face the situation, no matter what the outcome.

"Just a minute, Tina," she said. Cassi put away her pistol and unlocked the door.

"Come in."

Tina Colton walked into the living room. "Hi, Cassi." She said meekly.

"Hey, Tina. Please sit down."

"Thanks," She said, sitting on the couch as Cassi retrieved her coffee from the kitchen.

"Listen Cassi, I'm not gonna beat around the bush. I heard about Mick. I just came in from Malibu last night and was at his place watching the news, when two policemen came by and told me he was dead."

Cassi walked over and sat next to her friend. "Tina... I'm so sorry."

"It's not your fault," Tina put a hand on her friend's shoulder. " I'm sure you did all you could."

"I'm not done yet." Cassi said.

"Huh?"

Cassi took a sip of coffee. "I got a bullet into the one who shot Mickey and I'd know his face anywhere. Once I give his description to the station artist, I'm gonna check the files." Rage burned in her body like a white-hot fire and she trembled in spite of herself as she spoke through clenched teeth. "It's only a matter of time before I catch up with him, and when I do..."

Cassi let her words trail off into silence, having forgotten that Tina was listening to her and was surprised to see the younger lady's eyes wide with fear. She knew that fear all too well. It was the fear of losing the last person in the world who meant anything to you. She calmed down a bit. "I'm sorry, Tina," she said. "But Mickey meant a lot to me too, Y'know? He meant as much to me as you do."

Tears slowly ran down Tina's face. "I...I miss him. Oh, Cassi..."

Cassi hugged her tightly and as Tina's sobs shook her, she vowed, "I'll get those animals for you, Tina. I promise I'll get them."

Days later, after Mick's funeral, Cassi Day strode through the bustling confines of the Santa Bella Police department on her way to the precinct artist's office, the volley fired by the police in salute to Mickey echoing through her mind like the gunshot that had ended his life. The picture of Mick's killer was etched firmly in her mind and she wanted to get it on paper. No one bothered her during her trek, for they knew the fire of determination burning in those dark brown eyes. She'd just passed a small room with a coffee maker when she saw the artist, Ron Chase, filling his cup.

Standing five feet and nine and a half inches, Chase was a kid fresh out of college with a degree in art. He'd wanted to be a cartoonist, but there were no jobs available yet for his immense talent, so he used the police department as a stepping-stone until his dream was realized. Cassi stopped walking and leaned against the far wall, and hooked her thumbs into her jeans pockets, waiting for Ron to come out. When he emerged she called to him.

"Hey, Ron. Got a minute?"

"Oh hey, Cassi. Sure, what's up?"

"I got a little job for you," Cassi stood straight as Ron took a sip of his coffee. "I know who killed Mickey."

Her statement made Ron almost choke on his drink. He swallowed and looked at her. "That's great, Cass!" He said. "Who was it?"

"Well that's just it, Ron. I know the face but not the name." Cassi put an arm across Ron's shoulders. "That's where you come in. I need a quick sketch so I can see if it matches any of our mug-shots."

"Whew! That's a long-shot, Cass."

"Yeah, I know, but it's all I've got to go on for now."

Ron took another sip of coffee. "Well, let's get to it," he said, eagerly.

The two turned a corner and walked down four doors to Ron's small but neat office, which had several cartoon characters on its wall, most of which Cassi didn't recognize. But all were beautiful works of art. As she described the man she'd seen, Ron's brown eyes scanned the sketchpad and the pencil in his skilled hands worked a magic that awed Cassi, and she wasn't easily impressed. After just six minutes she had her sketch.

"Thanks, Ron." She said, admiring his work. "I owe you one."

She turned to leave, but Ron called her.

"Cassi?"

"Yeah, Ron?"

"I didn't know Mick as well as you, but he always treated me well. For what it's worth...you can thank me best by nailing this guy's hide to the wall."

Cassi put a hand on his shoulder and gave him a feral grin. "You got it." She winked at him and left the office.

Scorpio and Nick Freeman walked through the corridors of the Techno Computer Complex, discussing plans for future operations. For a while Freeman had something on his mind and was waiting for the right moment to ask his boss. When he could wait no longer, he spoke.

"If you don't mind my asking, sir," he said. "Why do you put up with an idiot like Rhodes?"

"True," said Scorpio. "He's an incompetent, spineless snail, but at least he keeps the police busy enough so they don't get too close."

"But the warehouse raid nearly fingered us, sir." The two men stopped at an elevator and Freeman rang for it. "He's already been shot, and we don't know for sure if any officers got a look at him or not. If the police catch up with him, he'll talk. He'll probably lead them right to us just to save his own gutless hide."

Scorpio glanced casually at his golden watch. He knew Freeman was right. Rhodes didn't have the fortitude to stick out a tough situation. He knew Rhodes would panic and then everything would turn sour. Rhodes had often tried to lie his way out of trouble when he'd messed up, but Scorpio had always seen through him. And if Scorpio could read him, the police would have no trouble in doing so either. "Then we'd better see to it that he doesn't do anything...foolish."

"Yes, sir." Said Freeman. "And what about this.... Cassi Day? If she is the officer who blew the Burbank Job, she could be trouble."

"You really think so, Rock?" Scorpio said, lightly amused at his henchman's urgency.

"With all due respect sir, yes."

"Ah, not to worry. If miss Day poses any threat, she'll be dealt with. The elevator came up and they got on, heading down to he lobby area.

Cassi spent hours reviewing the department mug shots, but found nothing so far to match the sketch. Disgusted, she stopped looking and decided to take a break.

"Lieutenant Day," She looked up to see the precinct Captain, Matthew Warden, standing in his office door. "I want to see you in my office. We've got some things to discuss."

Oh brother, this is all I need now, she thought. She got up and followed him into the office, where she closed the door behind her.

"Have a seat, detective," Said Warden, seating his six-foot three frame behind his desk. A father of two boys, Warden served the United States as a Ranger during the Vietnam War. After the war he became tired of being an instructor at Fort Benning and resigned from the Army. He became a police officer because it was the only job that complimented the leadership skills he'd developed as a soldier. Cassi sat on a small bench opposite the desk.

"How've you been holding up?" he asked.

"About as well as can be expected, Captain," she said, shrugging.

Warden leaned forward, resting his elbows on the desk. "Listen, Cassi, nobody knows better than me how tight you and Mick were. He was a damn good cop. He was like a son to me. But there's an official policy we have to go by in regards to cop killings."

Cassi crossed her legs and nodded her understanding, her eyes never leaving Warden's, but not really seeing or hearing him either. It was like she was looking through him at another time or place. "Right," she said.

"In other words, lieutenant, we can't go out there looking like we just opened up a revenge shop." Warden continued.

"Got it." She said, trying not to roll her eyes. She'd heard this speech several times before, but let Warden finish.

"So what's bothering you, lieutenant, besides losing your partner? Is there anything behind this thousand-meter stare you keep giving me?"

Cassi stood up. "What's bothering me, captain, is that Mickey's killer is still running loose out there some place, and I'm no closer to bringing him in than when this whole mess started. Think about it, sir. Didn't that drug cartel seem funny to you?"

"Funny?"

"Yes, sir. I mean we're talking about a street value of a million bucks, maybe even higher than that. This shipment wasn't anything like the cartels we've hit before. It was too big. I get the feeling we're dealing with some sort of syndicate."

"Interesting theory, lieutenant," said Warden. "And between the two of us, I believe you. Got any leads?

Cassi took a piece of paper from her back pocket unfolded it and handed it to the captain. "Only this, it's the guy who shot Mickey."

The captain took the sketch and examined it. "Anything matching our mug shots?"

Cassi shook her head. "Zip."

Warden handed the sketch and back to her. "Look's like you're fishing in the dark, lieutenant."

Cassi folded the sketch and put it back in her pocket. "I'm not gonna give up, sir. Something'll turn up somewhere."

" I don't think you ought to be involved in this case, lieutenant."

Cassi was astonished. "Why not?"

"Because you're half-cocked and ready to go out there, shooting up anything that moves. That's why. I've seen kids like you during the war. They didn't think or act rationally when their friends were killed and as a result, they were killed as well. I won't stand by and watch that happen to you too."

"With all due respect, sir, this isn't Vietnam. And besides, that was my partner, nobody else's. I have a right!"

Warden stared at her a moment. He knew there was no use arguing with her. Even if he put someone else on the case, Cassi would find some way to get mixed up in it. He knew that from past experiences. "All right, detective," He said. "You feel like you can handle this, fine. You crack this case and make it good for us. But you'd better watch your step, because department eyes are on you. And if you screw up, game over, got it?"

Cassi leaned forward, and placed both palms on Warden's desk. "You really know how to do a pep talk, don't you, cap?" She turned and opened the door and looked back at the captain. "It's too bad this isn't the old west."

Warden leaned forward. "Why's that?"

"Because when I caught Mickey's killer, I'd hang him."

Captain Warden grinned ruefully at her statement and returned to his paperwork, as she walked out of the office and disappeared into the busy throng of personnel.

CHAPTER 3

THE KILLER

Precinct Dispatcher, Natasha McKay, jogged briskly up the front steps of the police station. She'd switched shifts with a friend and was running a few minutes late. Five feet eight inches tall with red hair and green eyes, McKay was considered by many the classic Irish beauty, and she and Cassi had been good friends since their days at the police academy. She preferred something less intense than undercover work, which was why she became a dispatcher.

She'd just entered the double doors when Cassi walked up, on her way out. "Hi Cassi."
"Hey, how's it going, Natasha?"
"Not too bad," she said, checking her watch. "I'm running a bit late.
"You'd better hurry and clock in." Cassi said, grinning.
"Yeah, hey hang on a minute. I've got something to tell you."
"Okay."

Cassi moved back out of the way as the doors opened and other officers came and went, some of them speaking to her and she responded with a good-natured nod or a modest hi. She hooked a thumb in her jeans pocket and leaned on one hip, while she waited for her friend.

The doors opened again and two uniformed officers, one male and one female, entered carrying a struggling prisoner in tow. Before they got halfway down the hall, with him. The prisoner broke free and ran for the doors, with his captors in pursuit. Cassi stepped calmly into the charging prisoner's path, her arms folded. On and on he came, screaming maniacally and getting closer, but she stood her ground. As the prisoner reached for her with shackled hands, she fell on her side and opened her legs in a scissor-like fashion, closing them like a vice and trapping the prisoner's foot that stepped between them. Cassi quickly rolled over, causing the man to lose his balance and fall on his stomach. Before he could move, she was on top of him. Forming her hand into a knife, she viciously chopped him behind one ear, knocking him cold.

Cassi got to her feet and faced the two officers who were in charge of the prisoner. "Keys?" She said, panting slightly. The male officer tossed her the keys, while the female officer looked at her wide eyed with astonishment. Cassi unlocked the cuffs on one wrist and put the man's hands behind his back, again locking the cuffs. "He's yours," she said, tossing the keys back to them.

Awe struck, the two officers came over and pulled the stirring prisoner to his feet. "Thanks." Said the male officer, as the female nodded gratefully.

Cassi gave them a modest salute and they took the prisoner away, as Natasha walked over from where she'd been watching the whole spectacle.

"That was wild, Cassi," she said. "You've got to show me how to do that some day."

"You're on," said Cassi. "What did you want to tell me?"

"Huh? Oh, I never got to say how sorry I am about Mick. He was a good man."

Cassi grinned ruefully and nodded "That he was."

"If you need anything...you know my name."

Cassi hugged her friend and whispered, "Thanks, Natasha." Natasha patted her on the back and went to her post while, Cassi walked out the doors and down the steps to the back parking lot.

Jack Rhodes woke up from troubled sleep. Though he'd never been what people would call stable, he was jumpier and more nervous than ever since his meeting with Scorpio three weeks ago. Scorpio hadn't contacted him for another job yet, but Rhodes knew it was only a matter of time before he would. He didn't want to admit it, but Scorpio frightened him. Scorpio was a man of tremendous influence, intellect, and charisma, with vast connections and access to materials that no one even dreamed of, including Rhodes himself. And his connections made it easy for him to find his employees anytime and anywhere, which was why no one could ever leave the powerful Omega Syndicate.

Groggily Rhodes got out of bed and went to the hotel room kitchen for a beer. His arm bothered him a bit but not as badly as it had during his meeting with Scorpio. He was healing and was on medication for pain, but he didn't think a little beer would hurt. Rhodes grabbed a can from the refrigerator and closed the door. He sat back on the bed and opened the can and took a long drink. A loud noise like a gunshot came from outside, startling Rhodes so that he spilled some beer on himself. Wearing only a pair of lounge pants, he put on a robe and went over to the balcony and unlocked the patio door. Stepping outside, he looked over the railing at the scene below.

Amid the neon lights and throngs of people and vehicles, the noise sounded again. Rhodes looked harder and saw the smoking exhaust pipe of a red corvette that had backfired. He chuckled a bit at himself for being so jumpy. Rhodes downed the remnants of his beer and went back inside, glancing at the clock radio on the nightstand. It read 8:00 p.m. Inspired by the Santa Bella nightlife, he decided to shower, get changed and go out for a while.

The night was alive with activity as Cassi walked through the brightly lit, neon-studded streets in an area of the town she affectionately called "The strip." She was off duty and didn't feel like going home just yet, so she drove down to the strip to knock around for a while. Twisting through the throng of people, she made her way to LeChay's Cafe and went in.

The main area was dimly lit and speckled with tables, booths, and TV monitors. Off to the left was the bar and grill and to the right was small video game room. Cassi sought out a small table in a secluded part of the Cafe and sat down. When the waiter came, she ordered a grilled chicken sandwich and a coke. The waiter left to get her order and she watched the patrons around her to occupy her time. Some were talking, others smoking, others were laughing loudly at the bar and drinking, and she saw two couples kissing in the darker areas. Cassi grinned to herself and watched one of the TV monitors until her food came.

When she finished eating, a song she particularly liked came on from the jukebox. The song was "Her Town Too," which was appropriate because Santa Bella was her town. She loved everything about it. It's nightlife, the beaches, the surf...everything. She smiled again to herself and sipped the iced coke she'd ordered, totally soothed by the gentle melody of the song.

A bald man with muscular arms kept glancing at Cassi from was he sat at the bar. Though his arms were impressive his potbelly left much to be desired in regards to his being attractive. Sitting there in a gray tank top and brown slacks, he amusingly reminded her of the Kingpin in the Spiderman comics she'd read as a kid. The man finished drinking whatever was in his mug so fast that some of it leaked over the corners of his mouth and spilled onto his shirt.

Cassi sneered with disgust as the man belched loudly, wiped his mouth with the back of his hand, and came swaggering toward her table.

"Hey there, sweet thing," he said, flashing a snaggle-toothed smile that nearly made her stomach turn. "Buy ya' dinner?"

Cassi eyed him coolly. "No thanks. I just had my dinner." *Which I'm about to lose.* She thought, as she smelled him. He smelled so heavily of sweat and alcohol that Cassi thought she'd suffocate.

"If you're looking for a good time, I'm the man to see," he said, swaying a bit.

"I'll pass." Cassi said, annoyed.

"You don't know what you're missing, honey."

"Oh, really?"

Suddenly there came a sharp, metallic click from under the table, and the man looked down to see Cassi's pistol pointed at him. His eyes widened as he also saw the bronze officer's badge clipped to her belt.

"I don't think I'll miss anything at this range," she said.

The man looked at her eyes and knew she meant business. He turned nervously around and made his way back to the bar, while Cassi holstered her pistol. As other patrons entered the cafe, she tipped the waiter and got up to leave. She turned toward bar and felt her blood turn ice cold. There, seated on a stool and ordering a drink, was Mick's killer. There was no mistaking the triangular shape of his face, the pale blue eyes and the diagonal scar intersecting his left eyebrow. No mistaking the teased, blonde hair and five-foot ten-inch, rail-thin frame seated not quite fifty meters away from her. She didn't have to compare the sketch with what she was looking at...she knew it was him. Cassi stood rooted to the floor and as she stared at the man, a fiery rage flowed through her body like molten lava. All her muscles became tight springs, coiled and ready for action. Her vision clouded and she found herself looking at him through the red haze of her own anger.

She wanted to break every bone in his body, haul him downtown, and throw what was left of him in the cooler for life, If she could keep from killing him in the process. But even if she did haul him in, she'd have no case. Though she'd seen him gun Mick down, it would be her word against his, and she knew it. She'd been the only officer to see his face that night. With the greatest difficulty Cassi forced herself to calm down, and did only thing she could...keep an eye on him.

The killer ordered another drink and lit a cigarette, glancing nervously around from time to time as if he expected someone to jump him at any moment. If he'd known how close his suspicion came to being correct, he'd never have come to the cafe.

CHAPTER 4
ON THE TRAIL

The man stayed only twenty minutes before he was ready to leave. He paid for his drink, took a last drag on his cigarette before putting it out, and then left. Cassi slid out of her booth and followed him, stopping only to pick up an empty book of matches she'd seen him drop into the ashtray he'd been using. The name on the book was the Holiday Inn. She continued after him.

She tailed him down the block for eight minutes, careful not to lose him in the crowd, but keeping her distance so he wouldn't get suspicious. They continued on until they were nearly where she'd parked her car then Rhodes stopped short at a strip club called DOC's. Cassi walked past the club and sat on the hood of her car watching him as he paid the entrance fee and went in. She stood up and walked to the head of the line where a tall, muscular bouncer stopped her.

"Hold up, miss," he said, in a gravelly voice. "The line is behind you."

Without a word Cassi showed him her badge and ID card. Still he lingered. "Nice try, but I've seen fake badges before. My kid's even got one."

Cassi opened her jacket and revealed her pistol. "Your kid got one of these?" she snarled, her eyes flashing. "Look, the man you just let in is in danger and I'm assigned to protect him. You get in my way and something happens to him, I'll bust you for obstructing justice, got it?" Raising his hands in a gesture of surrender, the bouncer stepped back and let her in.

The house lights were down but the spotlight beamed brilliantly onto the large stage where a pretty, Latino girl danced to Robert Palmer's " Addicted To Love". The girl's top was already gone but when she took off the short, peach colored skirt, the place became a deafening crescendo of cheers, whistles, and shouts. The spectacle sickened and repulsed Cassi, as she stepped out of the isle and began looking for Rhodes. Her eyes scanned the room several times but she could find no trace of him. She angrily pounded her fist into her hand. *I'll murder that bouncer!* She thought. Glancing around one more, Cassi turned to go when she caught sight of a man slipping a dollar bill into the Latino girl's garter. It was the killer. Keeping her eyes locked on him, Cassi weaved her way through the tables filled with cheering, whistling men to another isle. She walked a third of the way down and took a seat in a dark area a few steps away from the isle. She could see him perfectly from there. He was seated at the corner of a short runway nearest the stage.

The song ended and the dancer blew the crowd a kiss and left the stage, wearing only black pumps and a pair of red panties, lined with dollar bills she'd gotten from the men. An announcer came on stage and said a few words then introduced the next dancer...Bianca. The men clapped and whistled some more as a very dark-skinned but lovely black woman, wearing a gray body suit, white boots, and black mini skirt came on stage and began dancing to George Clinton's "Atomic Dog".

Cassi glanced around at the howling mass of men and rolled her eyes. *If they'd just drop the word atomic from that song, it'd fit this bunch perfectly,* she thought. Hours later the bouncer came to the killer's table and said something Cassi couldn't hear above the crowd. He checked his watch, finished his drink, and then followed the man out of the room.

As they walked past her, Cassi bowed her head so they wouldn't see her. She inwardly cringed. What if the bouncer told the killer about her? Her cover would be blown and if he managed to escape her, he'd hide in a hole so deep she'd never find him again. She could've kicked herself for acting so impulsively. She'd let her thirst for vengeance cloud her thinking. There was nothing to do now but ride it out and hope for the best.

As soon as Cassi stepped into the isle follow them, a pair of rough hands gripped her buttocks and squeezed.

"Looking good there, baby cakes," said a patron, almost as skinny as the killer, with dark brown hair and round spectacles. "You dancing tonight?" Laughing, he wrapped one arm around her waist and tried to fondle her breasts with the other hand.

Enraged, Cassi stomped on the instep of his foot. She then elbowed him in the sternum, doubling him over. "Baby cake this!" she said, finishing him with a sidekick that sent him flying across one of the tables, knocking over other patrons and shattering a pitcher of beer. Another man, slightly shorter than the first but heavier and stockier in build approached her, reeking of liquor like the first man.

"That was my friend you just beat up!" he huffed.

"He asked for it!" Cassi shot back.

Screaming angrily, the man swung at her and she flung up her left arm and parried the blow, simultaneously grabbing his arm. Holding the trapped arm, Cassi stepped in and fired her elbow into the man's exposed side. She felt his ribs break under the force of the blow.

The waitresses screamed as a full-blown fistfight erupted with fists, bodies, and containers flying. The scene looked something out of a wild west movie as men bashed each other with chairs, fists and bottles while screaming waitresses and dancers ran in every direction trying to avoid getting hit. One dancer was hit in the back by a thrown bottle as she tried to get off the stage, and a waitress caught a stray fist to the temple that sent her sprawling to the floor.

Cassi made a break for the door as six bouncers ran in trying to restore order. She ducked out the door, just as a wine bottle crashed against it. Amid a crowd of frightened, confused patrons, the young officer searched the streets for the killer, but found no trace of him.

Minutes later, three police cars pulled up outside the building. Cassi counted six officers in all as they jumped out of their cars and made their way through the curious crowd of onlookers toward the club. She held up her police ID and badge as the first officer reached her.

"In there," she said, jerking a thumb backward.

The officer nodded and waved his men forward. "You okay?" he said.

"Yeah, I'm all right." Cassi said, brushing her hair back with her hand.

As the sergeant left to join his men, Cassi again scanned the streets for any sign of the man...nothing. It was as if he'd vanished into thin air. "Damn!" she whispered, angrily.

The killer had gotten into his rental car and headed for the highway. As promised, Scorpio had another job for him and he was excited. He didn't know what he'd be doing this time around, but he was glad to be back in action. Visions of the young Latino woman flooded his mind as he drove toward his destination. He'd managed to get her name. It was Conchita. He didn't know if that was her real name or stage name, but he planned to see her again.

Minutes later he was approaching Santa Bella's municipal airport, where one of Scorpio's private planes awaited him. Once he landed in Los Angeles, the syndicate boss sent a car for him and he was driven to the Techno Computer Complex. The parking lot was totally empty, except for three cars and four figures standing outside them. The unmistakable figure of Scorpio stood in the center, flanked by Freeman on the left and two Asian men he didn't recognize on the right. All were dressed in dark business suits. The driver stopped the car and the killer got out and walked toward the assembled men.

"Glad you could attend, " said Scorpio, in that cold, steely voice of his. He gestured to the men beside him. "This is mister Tsang, and this is mister Fu." Both men bowed almost simultaneously, as Scorpio looked back at his henchman. "They're interested in merging their opium business with ours."

"Okay, boss." said the killer, nodding.

Without another word, the men turned and walked toward the complex with the killer following. The elevator ride to the top floor, where Scorpio's office was, was a silent one and Scorpio noticed Freeman sneering at the killer, who was brushing lint from his Jacket. He used his peripheral vision to look at the two Asian men. If they noticed anything they kept silent. The elevator reached the top floor and the men disembarked and walked down the hallway toward Scorpio's office. When they reached it, Scorpio addressed the Asian men. "Gentlemen if you'd go in and make yourselves comfortable, I have some last minute matters to discuss with my men." The two men went inside leaving Scorpio alone with Freeman and the killer.

"Did you enjoy yourself tonight?" Scorpio asked the killer, nonchalantly.

He managed an embarrassed smile. "Wasn't anything, boss. I mean it was just something to do.

"I see...." Scorpio fixed his frigid glare on both men. "Gentlemen, I sense dissension within the ranks. Whatever differences you have, I suggest you resolve them quickly. This merger is very important to our business, and I don't have to tell you that any bickering among us not only destroys this transaction but ultimately the syndicate. And I won't tolerate that. Understood?"

"Yes, sir." Both men said, simultaneously.

"Excellent," said Scorpio. "If you would follow me?" The syndicate boss opened the door and the three entered the office.

"Dammit, Lieutenant, I just don't understand it!" boomed Warden as he paced back and forth behind his desk. "You weren't off duty four hours and you get mixed up in a fist fight! You mind telling me what you were doing in a strip joint last night?"

"I was following a suspect." Cassi said, from where she sat on the bench.

"What suspect?" said Warden.

"Mickey's killer."

Warden stopped pacing. "What?"

"You got it," Cassi said, sitting straight. "I knew it was him. I got a real good look at him the night he killed Mickey."

"Where'd you see him first?" Warden said.

"I'd just finished eating at a café when he came in and ordered a drink. I followed him to a night club and somebody sent for him."

Warden leaned forward and put both palms on his desk. "Who?"

"That's what I was gonna find out when this jerk decided to fondle me, and you know I wasn't gonna stand for that."

Warden folded his arms, his biceps bulging under his shirt. "No, I wouldn't either. But you could've handled the situation more delicately if the suspect meant that much to you."

Angrily, Cassi stood and walked slowly toward Warden's desk. "Yeah? How, give him a slap on the hand and say naughty boy?"

"You nearly broke those men in two!" Warden said.

"They'll heal." Cassi said, flatly.

Warden walked slowly around the desk toward Cassi, who stood with her arms akimbo as she watched him. "Lieutenant, I'm not sure I'm getting through to you. The public doesn't appreciate charges pending police brutality, justified or not! I've cut you some slack up till now, and I was skeptical about putting you on this case as it was. But if you push this too far, so help me I'll take your badge and your gun and lock you up myself!" He calmed down. "I'm not asking you to take smack from anybody. I just need to be sure that you're using your mind more than your fists, because if Internal Affairs gets wind of this, or it goes federal, then it'll be out of my hands, got it?"

"Yeah, cap," said Cassi.

"Did you get any more leads?"

Cassi reached into her jacket pocket and handed Warden the matchbook she'd found. "I saw him drop this in an ash tray before he left the café."

The captain examined the matchbook. He didn't have to tell her that there were several Holiday Inns in Santa Bella. Besides he knew she'd stake out all of them if she had to. She was just that determined. He gave her back the matchbook. "Anything else?"

Cassi thought for a moment. "Yeah, there are some people I know who might have some info I can use."

Warden nodded as he sat on his desk. "All right, lieutenant. Do what you gotta do, but remember what I said."

"You got it, cap." Cassi opened the door and walked down the hallway toward the parking lot.

CHAPTER 5

SHAKEDOWN

The killer boiled with anger as he flew back to Santa Bella. Though the meeting had gone well and preparations for the merger were under way, to his dismay he was still being used as a pick-up boy. A shipment of opium was due to arrive in Santa Bella in four days by ship and he was to pick it up and store it until Scorpio came to take charge. The irony of it all burned in his stomach like a red-orange poker. No matter what he did, he would always be looked at as a messenger...a go-for. It wasn't right! *I've been with this syndicate for years. I should be doing more than this!* he thought. He was sick of running himself to ground while Freeman lived it up as Scorpio's enforcer, a position that The killer thought he should've had years ago. No matter what it took, he'd find some way to get rid of Freeman.

Cassi drove toward the West End, which was the largest and most well known jazz café in western Santa Bella. Though mostly upper middle class and comfortably well off citizens frequented the café, the West End tended to attract a few shady characters from time to time. Cassi figured it wouldn't hurt to check things out, plus it would give her a chance to catch up with some friends of hers who worked there. Maybe they'd have some information she could use.

Turning left at an intersection, Cassi parked her car on the West End's lot and cut the engine. She locked the door behind her and casually checked her watch, as she strode toward the entrance. It was 3:30 pm. She grinned slightly to herself, knowing she'd come at a good time, for her friends' shift would end at 4:00 if any of them were working that night. The air smelled of sea and cooking meat and the sun's reflection threw off such a glare from the water that Cassi had to put on her sunglasses during her trek.

The smell of food, liquor, and cigarette smoke assaulted her nostrils as Cassi entered the café. Directly in front of her was the stage and lounging area and to her right was the bar and grill. On her left, studded with couches and small tables was a chat room, where a vast array of coffees, teas, and pastries were served. Cassi could hardly believe that just six months ago, the place was a movie theatre.

She'd removed her sunglasses and was about to go down into the lounge area, when a firm hand gripped her shoulder and a deep cold voice said, "Hold it, toots. I gotta check ya's for weapons before I let ya's in, see?"

Without looking around, Cassi calmly stated, "I always carry a weapon, Jim. You know that."

"How'd you know it was me?" Jim said, smiling."

Cassi turned to face her friend. "I 've got to admit, you nearly fooled me. Your acting skills are getting better."

"Well, I'm trying." Jim said, shaking her hand. "We're doing a 1930's play downtown tomorrow night and I'm one of the gangsters."

"Yeah? Well don't go getting slack on me, or I'll have to report ya's to da boss, ya get me?" Cassi grunted, doing her own gangster impression.

Jim stood with his mouth agape in astonishment for a few moments before saying, "That's great, Cassi. Where'd you learn to do that?"

"I grew up watching those old movies," Cassi answered, shyly. "Always did love a good gangster flick, and Bogey was my man."

"Aw, James Cagney would've creamed him." Huffed Jim, confidently.

"You wish!" Cassi said, playfully nudging him with her elbow.

The two friends laughed a bit before going to a more serious subject. "So, what brings you out this way, Cassi?" Jim said, sitting on a stool near the door.

"You know Mickey's dead?" she said, slowly.

"Yeah, I saw it on the news. I'm sorry."

"I've got a lead on the ones who killed him," Cassi said, placing her hands on her hips. "The trail's warm now, but if I don't get some fresh info, it's gonna go ice-cold, know what I mean?"

"Anything I can do?" asked Jim.

Reaching into her back pocket, Cassi pulled out the killer's sketch and handed it to her friend. "Ever see this guy before?"

Jim took the sketch and examined it briefly and then handed it back to her. "No, I've never seen him, but one of the girls might've." As patrons entered the café, Jim scanned the cocktail lounge area, where the waitresses were serving, until he found who he was looking for. "Chantal, could you come here a minute?" He called, waving to her.

The comely, ebony skinned, waitress put her tray on the bar and strode toward them, her light brown, almost hazel, eyes quizzically regarding Jim. When she saw Cassi with him, her tension eased and she smiled. "Cassi! What's up, girlfriend? Long time, no see." She said, hugging her.

"How's it going, Chantal. Good to see you."

Behind the two women, two men were engaged in a heated argument, which suddenly turned into a deafening shouting match of curses and obscenities.

"Uh oh, I'd better get down there before they come to blows," sighed Jim, as he stood.

"Need any help?" asked Cassi.

"Nope, I think I can handle it." And with that, the burly bouncer made his way through the circle of patrons surrounding the two potential combatants.

Chantal put her hands on her hips and said," Oh boy, there goes mister macho, showing off again. He doesn't have to do this to impress me."

Still watching the troublesome scene, Cassi folded her arms and said, "Didn't know you two were an Item."

"Well, I heard through the grapevine that he liked me, but he's actually shy around girls."

Cassi gave her friend a lopsided grin. "I never would've guessed."

Chantal blushed, slightly. "He's really sweet, but if he wants any kind of relationship with me, he's gonna have to come to me on his own. I don't go for the pony express routine."

"The pony express routine?"

"Yeah, you know, sending a friend over as a messenger? That's a major turn off for me."

Cassi nodded in acknowledgement then turned her attention back to the argument, which seemed to be getting worse by the minute.

Having placed himself between the two men, Jim calmly tried to suppress the melee that was about to take place. But the angry, drunken patrons wouldn't have it. The man behind Jim reached around him, swinging wildly, but Jim shoved him backward. The man staggered and fell down, while Jim wrestled with the first man, who'd picked up a chair. The fallen man climbed slowly to his feet, grabbed a wine bottle from one of the tables, and broke off the end, slowly advancing toward Jim and his antagonist.

Cassi had seen enough. She turned to Chantal. "Call the police. I'm going down there."

Chantal gently grabbed her friend's arm. "Be careful."

Cassi grinned recklessly at her. "You know me." She pulled her badge out and made her way toward the fracas. Another bouncer was plowing his way through the crowd across from her, but she could see he'd never reach Jim in time to help.

"Police!" She yelled. "Move! Get out of the way!" Breaking through the wall of spectators, the young detective flung herself between Jim and his attacker and kicked the bottle out of his hand. "Let's not make this any harder than it is," she said. "I don't want to hurt you."

In his drunken stupor, the man shook his head, blinked away his blurred vision, and stared blankly at her, while the second bouncer came onto the floor and grabbed him.

Cassi silently made her way through the crowd back to her friend. "I think Jim and company can handle things from here." She said, calmly.

Chantal sighed in relief. "Well, the police are on their way. And thanks for helping Jim out."

"Ah, no problem," Cassi said, waving her hand in light dismissal. Listen, Chantal, what I really want to talk to you about is this." She again pulled the sketch from her pocket and showed it to her friend. "This guy ever come in here?"

Chantal frowned in thought while she looked at the picture and then her eyes widened in recognition. "Wait a minute. Yeah, he was in here two nights ago."

"What happened?" Cassi asked, putting the sketch away.

"He was sitting at the table with two other guys. All of them were wearing business suits, but what separated him from the others was that he went for the Miami Vice look, sport jacket and slacks with dress shoes, but had a T shirt on instead of a formal shirt."

"Anything else?" asked Cassi.

"Yeah, he was trying to hit on one of the girls. I saw him talking to Janine when I was filling an order. I don't know what he said to her, but when I turned around, she slapped the fire out of him."

"Is that right?" Cassi said, folding her arms. "What happened after that?"

"Well, his friends laughed at him a bit and then they all left," said Chantal.

"Would you know him if you saw him again?" Cassi asked.

"I sure would," confirmed Chantal."

Cassi pulled her card from her jacket and gave it to her friend. "If you see him in here again, get hold of me either at the station or at home, okay?"

Chantal nodded. "Sure, Cassi."

Thanks, Chantal." Cassi hugged her friend and turned to go. When she reached the door, Jim called to her.

"Hey, Cassi, thanks for the save."

"Any time." She called back, waving. Cassi went to her car, started it up, and drove away.

During her drive, She couldn't help but feel a bit disappointed. Though she'd gotten some information, none of it got her any closer to what she was looking for. The trail was getting colder. She had to think of something, anything that would broaden her lead. Then she thought of "Slide." Of course! Why hadn't she thought of him sooner? He'd been a key informant to both her and Mickey. If she hurried to the strip, she just might catch him."

At the intersection of 23rd and Pickett, just one block west of the strip, the man known as "Slide" sat at a bus stop smoking a cigarette, since he had a little time to kill before he went to work. To see him sitting there in his leather jacket and matching cap, faded blue jeans, and converse sneakers, no one would've guessed he was a bartender. And though he made good money at his profession, he preferred to dress conservatively, so as not to draw unwanted attention to himself.

Having finished his smoke, he dropped the butt to the ground and mashed it under his foot. He stood and stretched and started toward the strip and the Rocky Mountain Pub, where worked, when he heard a car horn sound. "Slide" turned around and saw a blue Trans AM pulling out of traffic toward him. The car parked next to him at the curb. A door opened and Cassi Day stepped out.

"Yo, Slide, what's in the breeze?" she chimed.

"A little bit of everything, doll. Can you dig it?"

"I sure can," Cassi said, leaning against her car. "You punching in tonight?"

"Yeah, just for a few hours," answered Slide.

Cassi gestured to her car. "Jump in and I'll jet you over there.

"I appreciate that, sugar cube." Slide said, walking toward the car.

Cassi leaned inside and unlocked the door for him and then put on her seatbelt, as he got in the car. The ride was a short one and Slide still had some time to kill before he punched in, so Cassi took this opportunity to get some info from him. Locking the car doors, She and Slide went into the pub, which was alive with action. Some people were playing darts, others listening to the jukebox, while still others were huddled over drinks at various tables.

Seeking out a secluded table, Cassi motioned for Slide to follow her and sat down. They spoke in Santa Bella-style slang to confuse any potential eaves' droppers.

"So, Slide, any smoke blowing your way?"

"And you know it," Slide answered. "And it's so thick I can't see my hand in front of my face, dig it?"

Cassi grinned slightly, knowing that she'd hit the jackpot. "Can a girl get a hit?"

"Roll up your sleeves, doll 'cause the doctor's gonna make you feel all right." Slide said, leaning a bit closer. "There's been some heavy dudes from out of town playing some serious hardball hereabouts, drumming up snow like nobody's business, follow me?"

"Yo, out of the trenches, and straight to the front lines, baby," purred Cassi. "Keep shooting."

"Right on, and bust this...Static on the box is that there's gonna be a hook up between these out of town boys and your boy, Turk, in two days."

"Turk? You're jazzing me." Cassi said, with an accusing look.

"No jazz, doll. He's caught up in the gears somehow."

Cassi thought for a moment and then slowly shook her head in disbelief. " I thought he was still in the slam."

"No dice, angel," Slide said, holding up his hands in an "I don't know" gesture. "He got time off for good behavior."

Cassi nodded. "So, where's the bomb gonna drop?"

"Larsen's Laundromat, around noon."

"Straight?"

"Straight up, angel, no jazz." Slide said, coolly.

Cassi gave Slide a soul handshake, placing a folded twenty dollar bill into his hand as she did. "Thanks for the info, knew you wouldn't leave me hanging."

As they got up from the table, Slide said, "Hang on a second and I'll stand you to a drink."

"Okay." Cassi said. She walked over and leaned against the bar, as Slide went to the back to punch in. While she waited for him, a man dressed in brown slacks and a gray bomber-style jacket approached her.

"What's a nice girl like you doing in a place like this?" he asked, tilting back the gray fedora on his head.

Cassi wanted to laugh. She'd heard that pick up line a million times. Turning to face him, she leaned backward with her elbows resting on the bar.

She had to admit that he was quite handsome. He was tall and slender and had a good build, but what got Cassi's attention were his brown eyes, which had a playful but somewhat reckless set to them. He looked like the black version of Indiana Jones. She knew what he was after, but decided to play the game a bit.

Slightly cocking and eyebrow, she said, "I'm not that nice." Her voice was a sensuous purr.

The man looked intrigued. "Got a wild side to you, huh?"

Cassi nodded. "Umm hmm."

Just then, Slide returned to the bar with a can of soda. "Think fast, angel." He called, sliding the coke can down the bar to her, hence his nickname.

Using her peripheral vision, Cassi flicked her wrist, opened her hand, and caught the sliding beverage. "Thanks, Slide. See ya' around." She said, winking at him.

"You're pretty well known around here too, aren't you?" The young man said, impressed."

"You might say I'm a regular."

"That guy called you angel. Is that your name?" He asked, as they walked out to the parking lot.

"That's what some people call me." Cassi answered.

"Y'know, I swear I've seen you somewhere before," said the man. "Where do you work?"

Cassi unclipped her badge and showed it to him.

Astonished, the man looked at her. "C'mon, babe, is this thing real?"

"Uh huh," She said, softly. "And so is this." Cassi calmly opened her jacket just enough to reveal her pistol.

"Jeez! You're a cop?"

Smiling, Cassi nodded in affirmation, and the man pulled his hat brim down over his eyes, put his hands in his pockets, and walked nervously back into the pub. Stifling a giggle, Cassi walked back to her car and got in. Still grinning, she drove into the night.

Cassi parked her car in an alley across the street from a recently closed Laundromat in the bay area. According to Slide, this was where the deal was supposed to take place. She cut the engine and leaned back on the seat, chewing a stick of gum, while she waited for her suspects to arrive. The noon sun warmed the spring day so much, that she took off her jacket and opened the car door to let some air circulate through it. Moments later a yellow dodge charger pulled onto the Laundromat's parking lot, and Cassi quickly pulled the door shut and lay across the front seat to escape notice. She rose to where she could just see over the dash-board and there was her suspect, Turk, looking like he'd just stepped out of the seventies with his bell-bottom slacks, brown vest and white long-sleeved shirt, rolled up a the wrists. Turk carried a black brief case and was flanked by two men wearing T-shirts and jeans with pistols in their waistbands. Turk saw her car, but didn't think much of it. For all he knew, some teens ran out of gas and left it there while they went for fuel. The trio walked up the stairs and entered the building.

Cassi slowly shook her head. "Turk, Turk. When will you ever learn?" She'd started to sit up, when a black Cadillac pulled onto the lot and four men in business suits got out and headed for the building. Cassi ducked back down and watched as they vanished into the Laundromat as well. When she was sure no more people were coming, she got on the radio and called for back up. She then got out of the car and crept over to the entrance. Jerking her Beretta from the shoulder holster, she checked the clip, chambered a round, and then eased inside.

The room was dark and silent, except for the sound of muffled conversation as Cassi made her way through the area. She moved silently behind empty racks and carts, keeping her ears open for conversations. At first she saw nothing but as she peered harder, she saw the suited men conversing with Turk and his men. Unable to hear their conversation, she edged around yet another rack and maneuvered her way toward them like an army commando behind enemy lines. Peering over a clothing cart, she saw the men moving toward a freight elevator. When she heard the elevator doors close, she got up and ran to it to check the floors. It stopped on the third floor. Cassi looked around and found a stairwell, exited the room, and started up the stairs. She could hear the men talking as she made her way up the last flight to the door atop the stairs. She opened the door to a mere slit and looked inside. To her left was a small, dead-end hallway filled with empty clothing carts, and a short distance to her right was a corner. Slipping into the hallway, she flattened herself against the wall and eased to the corner and peeked carefully around it, her weapon ready.

Turk was seated at a wooden table with his men at this side while the suited men stood in the front of him in a half circle. He opened one of the clear bags in the front of him, dipped a finger into it, and licked the white powder off it. "Whoooo!" he yelled, happily. "This stuff is pure!"

"It's genuine alright," said one of the suited men, impatiently. "Now... the money." As Turk reached for his briefcase, some of the suited men fingered their pistols. Turk's men did the same.

"Easy now, gents," said Turk, raising his hands. "Here's your cash, like we agreed." One of the suited men took the case and Cassi watched silently as he counted the money, her heart pounding with excitement.

"It's all here," said the man.

"Sure it is," said Turk. "You don't think I'd hold out on Scorpio, do you?"

"I wouldn't advise it." Warned another of the suited men.

Cassi thought about the name she'd just heard. "Scorpio?" She moved quietly back down the stairs then took off like a shot through the facility. Bursting through the exit door, the young detective vaulted over the short balcony to the ground and ran across the parking lot toward her car. She'd just reached the sidewalk, when a plain-clothed policeman signaled her. It was her friend, Nick Johnson. "Hey, Cassi. We came as soon as we got the word."

"Good, how many men did you bring?"

"Six, including myself," said Nick.

Cassi quickly gave the descriptions of all the suspects to her friend and he went back to the van he'd arrived in and relayed the message to the other officers. The officers, all in civilian clothes, then got out and positioned themselves near the building. Nick gave Cassi a small two-way radio and she went back inside and hid downstairs until the transaction was over. When the suited men came out of the elevator, Cassi whispered into the radio, "Here they come. Take 'em!" The men were arrested the instant they stepped into the streets. When the suited men were secured, Cassi spoke to Nick.

"I'm gonna need two of your men," she said.

"You got' em. Harris, Bronson, go with her."

"Let's go!" she said, waving them forward. Pistols drawn, the officers followed her into the facility. Cassi whispered to the officers, "I want you two to post this room. There are three guys upstairs and they're packing heat. If any of them get past me, take them alive if you can." And with that, Cassi ran up the stairwell.

When she reached the third floor, she wasn't surprised to see that Turk and his men were still there, knowing Turk's drug habit. Having taken a razor blade and cut off a section of coke, Turk was sniffing it through a straw while his men looked on. Neither of them noticed as Cassi slipped out of the stairwell and into the hallway. Weapon at the ready, she cautiously eased toward them, adrenaline coursing through her. The men were laughing and talking so loud that they were caught completely off guard when Cassi walked casually around the corner, pointed her weapon, and said, "Remember me, Turk?"

Turk's eyes widened in surprise and fear as he beheld the Amazon-like figure glaring down at him. "Oh Jeez!" he cried, as his men fumbled for their weapons.

One of Turk's men was faster than she'd anticipated and had his weapon out almost before she could blink. But Cassi fired quickly, hitting him in the gun hand. The hoodlum fell to the floor clutching his shattered wrist while Turk's second man fired at her. The room echoed with a resounding boom, as yellow-white flame blossomed from the gunman's barrel. The bullet snapped past Cassi's left ear, and blew out the window behind her.

Cassi ducked low and somersaulted forward. While on her back, she pushed upward with her feet, kicking the table toward the startled men and spilling cocaine onto the floor. Turk was extremely agile and managed to get out of the way, but his henchman wasn't as lucky. He staggered backward, slipped on one of the bags of coke, and fell with a thud while Turk made a break for a sub hallway in back of the room. Cassi jumped to her feet, ran over and kicked the gun out of the fallen man's hand before he could use it again. She then knelt down and flattened him with a rabbit punch to the temple.

"You have the right to remain silent, Jerk!" She said to his unconscious form.

Turk had made it to the mouth of the hallway when he spun around and shot at Cassi with his own pistol, missing her by a mile. She fired back, and her bullet buried itself into the wall next to Turk's head. Turk took off down the hallway at a dead run with Cassi behind him. She stopped at the hallway opening, peeked around the corner, and then ducked back as Turk fired again, his bullet hacking out a chunk of concrete where her head had been. He continued running until he came to a section of hallway studded with huge windows. He kicked one of them out and jumped to a lower section of roofing.

As he rolled to his feet he saw that Cassi had reached the window he'd just jumped from and jumped to an even lower roof. Cassi followed Turk's lead, jumping to lower roofs when she saw him aim at her again. She fell into a prone position, as he fired yet again. The bullet glanced off a pipe above her and went screaming into the distance. Cassi looked over the roof's edge and saw Turk running toward a Larsen Company pickup truck parked on another section of the lot. She got to her feet and resumed pursuit. Turk started the truck just as Cassi jumped to the ground and came racing toward him. Throwing the gear into reverse, he hit the accelerator, causing the vehicle to go into a hundred-and-eighty degree spin. He then switched to drive and floored the accelerator. Cassi had nearly reached the truck when it roared off toward a chain-link fence. Barely three feet away, and without breaking stride, she dove forward, grabbed the tail gate, and hung on for dear life as the truck smashed through the fence and screeched into traffic.

Horns blared and tires squealed as vehicles swerved to keep from hitting the young woman being partially dragged behind the speeding truck. Ignoring the mind-numbing pain in her arms, which had nearly been pulled from their sockets when she'd grabbed the tailgate, Cassi pulled herself up and got a foothold on the back bumper. She was just about to climb over the rear when Turk suddenly hit the breaks to avoid a car and dodged right. The sudden motion flipped her over the tailgate and she landed on her back on the floor. The truck swerved again violently throwing her to one side, where she banged her head painfully against the side of the Truck.

Hearing noise behind him, Turk looked back and his eyes popped in disbelief as he saw Cassi lying stunned in the back of the truck. *You gotta be kiddin' me!* He thought. *This chick's crazy!* He turned back around and dodged left just barely in time to miss a cement mixer. Cassi shook her head, blinked away her blurring vision, and rolled over onto her hands and knees. Getting to her feet she climbed on top of the speeding vehicle and laid prone, her arms outstretched and hands gripping the top of the truck at the windows. The truck suddenly made a sharp left turn, pulling out of traffic onto a small two-lane road and Cassi held on for all she was worth, as centrifugal force nearly pulled her off the Truck.

"Whoooooa!" she cried, her heart pounding as the wind whipped through her long hair and blurred her vision. *Maybe this wasn't such a great idea after all!* she thought.

Hearing sirens behind her, Cassi looked back and saw two police cars and a motorcycle cop chasing them. They were a few minutes away yet, but were rapidly closing the gap. Turk heard the sirens as well and reached for the automatic in his back waistband in desperation, having emptied revolver at Cassi. He knew he couldn't hit any of the cops chasing him just yet, so he turned his attention back to Cassi. After all she'd been he reason he'd spent two years in prison. What better way or time to get revenge? Chambering a round, Turk pointed the gun upward and fired.

Cassi gasped as five bullets tore through the roof of the truck just inches away from the ribs on her right side. Grabbing the cargo lights in front of her, she pulled herself forward just barely evading another barrage of gunfire. She swung her body around so that she now faced the windshield while she gripped the truck's hood. Turk pointed his weapon at Cassi and pulled the trigger, causing her to reflexively duck, but the bolt locked forward, indicating an empty magazine. Throwing the weapon aside in disgust, he stomped the accelerator, whipping left and right, trying unsuccessfully to get rid of the woman clinging to the hood.

Turk hung a sharp left and steered into a huge construction site. The police were almost right behind them as they entered the site, their sirens deafening. As the truck bounced along the sandy ground Cassi looked back and saw the truck was headed straight for the Iron girders of an uncompleted structure. "See ya, babe!" shouted Turk as he opened he door. He hesitated a moment, then jumped out of the truck. Cassi rolled off the hood and hit the ground rolling as the speeding vehicle smashed into the girders, sending fragments of metal and glass in all directions. Recovering from the fall, she struggled to her feet and saw Turk running across the site. The policemen jumped from their vehicles and came running toward her. She was surprised to see that one of them was none other than Captain Warden himself. All men had their guns drawn when they reached her. "You okay, lieutenant?" asked Warden.

"Yeah," she said, panting. "But I gotta catch..." Cassi looked at the motorcycle officer's bike and thought of the head start Turk had. "Mind if I borrow your bike, Charlie?"

"Not too much breakage huh, Cass?" said Charlie.

"Thanks, Charlie, you're a sweetie." Cassi mounted the bike, jumped on the kick-starter, and roared off in the direction she saw Turk going.

"Follow her!" yelled Warden, waving the officers toward the patrol car.

Cassi caught sight of Turk turning toward a half completed building and sped after him, racing past the officers chasing him on foot.

Panting with sheer exertion, Turk ran as if very devil himself had risen from hell and was after him. And remembering Cassi Day's interrogation methods, he knew that wasn't far from the truth. Cassi was a devil...a she-devil, and Turk knew that from his first encounter with her. Now here he was again running from the same officer who'd brought him down before.

Weaving between the half-built structures Cassi cut in front of him and slowed him down. In trying to change direction, Turk stumbled and fell but was up and running again almost instantly. Cassi cut the bike's engine got off and sprinted after him, gaining with every step. She tackled him around the waist and crashed him to the ground and they scrambled in the dust a tangle of arms and legs as Warden and his men stopped just a few feet from them. Turk crawled on his stomach trying to get away, but Cassi knelt on his back and wrenched his arms behind him, cuffing his wrists. She hauled him to his feet and read him his rights as Warden and his men arrived.

"See ya' later, Turk," said Cassi, as the officers took him away. "We got a lotta catching up to do...babe." She sat on the hood of the patrol car as Warden addressed her.

"What happened here, lieutenant?"

"This was one of the contacts I told you might be able to help me out," said Cassi.

"That junkie?"

"Yeah, he deals in coke and I figured he'd know where any shipments would be coming in"

Warden put his hands on his hips. "Any other secrets you're holding out on me?"

"Me, sir?" she said, innocently.

"Forget I asked," Warden said, throwing up both hands. "C'mon let's get this guy booked."

CHAPTER 6

A BIGGER PIECE OF THE PUZZLE

Turk sat in the police interrogation room nervously fidgeting with his hands. He'd played this game before and he silently prayed that different officers would question him this time. He kept stealing fearful glances at Cassi, who was standing outside the window in the hallway talking to Warden. During the two hours since Turk's capture, Cassi had gone home, showered, changed and tended to the bumps and bruises she'd gotten during the chase. Now here she was discussing facts and theories about the drug bust.

"How long are you going to let him sweat?" said Warden, glancing at Turk through the window.

"Just playing it cool for now," Cassi said. "I'll give him a few more minutes. Where are those other guys we nailed?"

"They're in another part of the station."

Cassi folded her arms and leaned against the wall. "Any of them talk yet?"

Warden shook his head.

Cassi was silent for a while, deep in thought and piecing the whole incident together. "Something about this doesn't fit the picture."

"What's that?" said Warden.

"I've known Turk for years and he's just a small-time hustler, not a real bad guy, just can't leave drugs alone. When I busted him a couple of years ago, he didn't put up much of a fight, but today he was more aggressive than I've ever seen him."

"All the more reason to put him away." said Warden, drinking the last of his coffee.

Cassi shook her head and looked at her captain, her eyes locked on his. "No, I think he's afraid somebody might ice him if he talks to us."

"Any idea who?" said Warden.

"I heard him mention somebody called Scorpio. I believe that's his drug supplier. Does that name ring a bell to you?"

Warden thought for a moment, then looked back at her and shook his head.

Cassi nodded and glanced back at Turk, who was still fidgeting. "Let's go have a little talk with our guest." She opened the door beside the window and Warden followed her into the interrogation room.

William Thompson withdrew the last of his savings from the bank and hurried out to his car and the pretty brunette fiancé who waited for him. He jumped in the car and rubbed her legs as she gave him a passionate kiss. Though the Techno Computer Company paid a decent salary, he'd gotten a better offer from another company in Colorado and had given his two weeks notice. All he could think about was his wife to be and the new life he'd begin once he reached Colorado. Thompson started his car and drove out of the parking lot.

When he was far out of the city, he turned the car down a winding two-lane road. He negotiated his first turn and that's when he realized his breaks were gone. How could this have happened? The breaks worked fine earlier, and he was only in the bank for eight minutes. But then he remembered his fiancé had gone to the restroom for a few minutes. And with no one inside, someone could've had ample time to sabotage the car. But why, he'd done nothing to anyone. Who would do this?

Thompson had no time worry about any of that now as he frantically tried to keep the now out of control vehicle on the road. The car swerved from side to side and Thompson's terrified fiancé shrieked as she clutched his arm, her screams nearly bursting his eardrums. Thompson looked up and saw a hairpin curve with a steep slope jutting out to the side, which prevented the curve from being a sheer drop. But even so, the incline was so steep that nothing would prevent the car from turning over if they went over the side. But for the moment they still had a chance. The ground around them was fairly level. If they could jump before they hit he curve...

Keeping one hand on he wheel, Thompson reached over unbuckled his fiancé's seatbelt. "Rachel, jump!" He shouted. But Rachel by now was so hysterical with fright that she didn't even hear him. The ground was rapidly giving away to steepness as they neared the curve. Thompson tried desperately to pry Rachel's hands from his arm and control the car, but couldn't do either. The curve was right in front of them and he steered toward the rocky hillside to avoid it, but another car came around the curve and smashed headlong into Thompson's car.

Rachel's head smashed hard against the windshield and she slumped over, unconscious. Thompson's ribs and sternum had been crushed by the steering wheel and he tried vainly to call out to his fiancé, blood oozing from his mouth. Having been knocked backward by the crash, the car listed to one side, and in a final horrifying moment, Thompson knew he was going over the side. The car bounced down the slope, rolling over several times before it hit the bottom and burst into flames.

High above the gruesome scene floated a helicopter. Lower and lower it came, its occupants observing the destruction below. The chopper's radio came to life, and the co-pilot answered. "This is whirly bird."

Scorpio's cold voice came over the radio. "Mr. Freeman, what's the status of our former employee?"

"Retired, sir...permanently," said Freeman, still looking at the smoldering wreckage.

"Excellent," said Scorpio. "Return to the compound."

"Roger, on my way," said Freeman, tapping the pilot on his shoulder. "Let's go." The chopper slowly ascended then flew off into the distant skies as black smoke billowed up from the flaming wreckage below.

"Let me lay it on the line for you," Cassi said, sitting on the table next to Turk. "As it stands, things aren't looking so good for you, honey. Possession of drugs with intent to distribute, resisting an officer, possession of an illegal firearm, assault with intent to commit murder, not to mention half a dozen traffic violations." Cassi shook her head. "With charges like these, the judge is gonna Jack that prison up and set it on top of you, know what I mean?"

Turk glanced up at Cassi then his eyes fell to his fidgeting hands. "What do ya' want from me?"

"Who's Scorpio, Turk?" Cassi said.

"I...I don't know what you're talking about." Turk said, nervously.

"Don't play with me," she warned "I heard you say something about not holding out on Scorpio when you were talking' to those other goons we caught. I want to know who or what this Scorpio is!"

"Son, you've got enough charges against you to put you away for life, so I advise you to start talking," said Warden from where he stood near the door, his arms folded.

"Either way you're going to jail, but if you give us any information that'll help us finger these guys, it might knock some time off your sentence," said Cassi.

"Y-you don't know what they'll do. I can't mess with them!" "Even in jail I'm a dead man!"

The urgency in his voice and terror in his eyes confirmed her suspicions. She got off the table and walked over to Warden. "Sir, would you give me a few minutes alone with him?" she whispered. "I'm sure he knows more than he's letting on."

"What if you're wrong, lieutenant?" whispered Warden.

"It won't be the first time, sir." Cassi said, shrugging.

"Don't hurt him." Warden warned.

"Don't worry." Cassi assured, winking.

Warden opened the door and left the room and fear exploded through Turk. "Where you goin'? D-don't leave me alone with her!" He called after the Captain, but Warden disappeared. Cassi closed and locked the door then turned to her terrified prisoner.

"It's just us now," she said, walking slowly toward him. "I want answers, Turk. You'd better start talking and I'm not even close to kidding!"

Turk got up and backed away from her. "Look, t-they'll kill me if I talk to you!"

"Who will, Turk, Scorpio? He's your supplier, isn't he?"

"Y-yes!" Turk stammered. Cassi kept walking toward him.

"What else?" Turk had backed himself into a corner in the small room. There was nowhere to go and no way out except through Cassi, and he knew better than to try and fight her. "What else, Turk?" she repeated. "I'm not gonna ask you again."

"Okay, okay," said Turk. "Those guys you caught don't usually make the deliveries. It's usually just one guy."

"What does he look like?" she said, stopping.

"Blonde hair, blue eyes, kinda' skinny." The description sounded familiar and Cassi pulled the sketch out of her pocket, unfolded it, and showed it to Turk. "Does he look like this?"

"Yeah, yeah that's him all right." Turk said.

"What's his name?"

"I heard somebody call him...Rhodes."

"You're sure about this?"

"Yeah, it was one of the guys with him, who called his name."

Cassi folded the sketch and put it away. "These guys you talked to today, were any of them with Rhodes any time he delivered the goods?"

"Yeah, one of them was."

"All right," said Cassi. "We're gonna put them in a line up and you show me which one."

"N-no!" cried Turk, panic-stricken. "Are you crazy? They'll know I turned them in!"

Cassi put her hands on her hips "Look, you got nothing to worry about. They'll be behind a glass. You can see them, but they can't see you."

Turk looked skeptical. "I'm just supposed to believe that?"

Cassi went to the door and looked outside the window. She tapped the window glass to get the attention of the officer passing by and beckoned him while she unlocked the door. When the officer stepped in, she leaned close and whispered something to him that Turk couldn't hear then left the trooper to stand guard while she disappeared down the all in the same direction Warden had gone. Minutes later she returned with Warden behind her. The officer moved aside as she opened the door and said,

"On your feet, Turk. We're gonna take a little walk."

"What are you gonna do?" asked Turk, apprehensively. Without a word, Cassi walked in, and took hold of one of Turk's arms, and pulled him to his feet. She cuffed his hands behind him and led him to the door. "Thanks for your help." She said to the uniformed officer, who waved and left the room.

They led him past several staffed cubicles and down a flight of stairs to a hallway just wide enough for the three of them to walk side by side. Passing several small offices, they turned left at the end of the hallway and went down some steps into a small, dark room resembling an auditorium with an isle down the center and chairs on both sides facing a wall, which held a long window. Above the window was a thick, white shade and off to the left was a small, wooden table with a radio console on it. Striding down the isle, Cassi went through a door to the right of the long window and hit the light switch inside to reveal a small stage with five black, eight-foot lines painted on the white wall behind it, and above each line the numbers one through five were painted in order from left to right. As Cassi came back through the door, Warden led Turk down the isle where she unlocked his handcuffs. The police captain then took the prisoner into the line up room and positioned him on the opposite side of the window. Cassi pulled the small table over and placed it just under the window. Turning the console on, she keyed the handset and thumbed the talk button.

"Can you hear me in there?" she said.

Warden turned on the intercom. "Say again?"

Cassi chuckled a bit before speaking. "Can you hear me?"

"Loud and clear," answered Warden, turning to Turk. "Whatever she says, do the opposite, got it?" Turk nodded, nervously.

Cassi pulled one of the chairs to the table and sat down. Keying the handset again, she said, "Okay Turk, raise your right hand." Remembering Warden's instruction, Turk raised his left hand. "That's your left hand, Turk," Cassi said. She pulled her pistol from her shoulder holster. Checking to make sure the safety was on, she pointed the weapon at him through the window. "Captain would you bring him in here a moment?"

As he entered the room, Turk froze in mid stride when he saw Cassi's pistol pointed right at him. She twirled the gun on her index finger like a western gunfighter then shoved it back into the holster. "Didn't see that, did you?" she said, with a wicked grin. Warden had seen her weapon too and came pushing in behind Turk.

"Have you lost your mind, lieutenant?"

"No, sir," she stated, calmly. "Just proving a point."

"I wonder about you sometimes, detective...I really do," said Warden. Hearing a thudding sound, both officers looked down to see that Turk had fainted.

Scorpio watched from his office window as Freeman's chopper landed on the building's roof. With his hands clasped behind him, he walked slowly from behind his desk and waited for his lieutenant. Within minutes there was a knock at the door. "Enter," he said. The door opened and Freeman casually walked in.

"Neatly done, Mr. Freeman," said Scorpio." "I trust your other assignment was equally well executed?"

"Yes, sir," Freeman confirmed. "Everything's been arranged."

"Have a seat, Mr. Freeman. There's been a change of plan," he said, gesturing to one of the two chairs in front of him. Freeman walked over and sat down as he continued, "When the shipment comes in I want you to go to Santa Bella, evaluate the situation, and take over from there." Freeman nodded his understanding. "This operation is too important for a simpleton like Rhodes to try to handle. I want a man I can count on out there."

"Understood, sir." Said Freeman.

"Good, now we'll go over phase two after the cartel's in place." Freeman leaned closer listened, as the Syndicate boss commenced with the plans.

During the past hour Cassi had interrogated the suspect identified by Turk. She'd gotten very little from him, but even that little bit got her closer to what she was after, The information she'd gathered didn't get her any closer to Scorpio, but when asked about Rhodes the man had said, "Jack? He's nothing, just a big shot wanna be." At that point, Cassi strategically ended her interrogation, for now she had the full name of Mick's killer. She put his name in the computer to check for any aliases he might have used and found six.

On her way to her desk another officer called to her. "Hey, Day, call for you."

"Well, who is it?" she said.

"Hey, what am I, your secretary?"

"Yeah, it's probably your weave," replied Cassi, causing most of the other officers to laugh. She went over to her desk and hit the hold button, as she picked up the phone. "Lieutenant Day," she said.

"Cassi, it's Tina."

"Hey Tina, sorry I couldn't get back to you sooner but I've been pretty busy."

"So I gather," said Tina. "Find anything yet?"

"I found a lot, but I can't talk here. I'll fill you in when I get home, Okay?"

"Sure, Cassi." Tina said. "See you then."

They hung up and Cassi sat at her desk to write her reports. When she finished, she went over and knocked on Warden's door. "Come in," he said, looking up from the reports he was reading. Cassi came in and handed the reports to Warden. Though she had mastered the art of not showing weakness, the Captain could see the fatigue and stress in her eyes. "Here you go, sir," she said. "Everything's in order."

Warden accepted the reports and put them on his desk. "Have a seat, detective." He said, gesturing to the bench in front of his desk. Cassi closed the door and sat down as Warden continued. "Now that you've got a name and face to go on, what are your intentions?"

"I'm gonna have another talk with Turk, she said." I want to see if I can lure Rhodes into the open."

"How do you intend to do that?"

"Simple, I'll get Turk to contact Rhodes and set up another delivery and when he shows, I'll nail the coffin shut."

"And if that doesn't work?"

"I'll start checking' hotels with this list of aliases I dug up." She handed the list to Warden. "He's bound to have used one of those fake names."

"Even if you do catch him that way, lieutenant, you still won't have anything to go on except mere suspicion. "Warden handed the list back to her.

"That's why I'm hoping my first plan will get him," she said, putting the list away.

"You look like you're ready to collapse, lieutenant, "Warden said. "You've been running yourself to death ever since this whole thing started. You really need to get some rest. This case isn't going anywhere."

Cassi nodded wearily, knowing the captain was right. "Okay, anything else?"

"That'll be all for now, "Warden said. "Get some rest, lieutenant, and that's an order."

Cassi stood and saluted. "Yes, sir."

Tina was asleep when Cassi came in that night. She'd been watching TV and hand gotten drowsy while waiting for her friend to return. Cassi turned off the TV and walked to the kitchen for a drink. Pulling a can of TAB soda from the refrigerator, she popped the top and went back to the living room and slumped wearily into a chair next to the couch, where Tina lay curled up. As Cassi drank the soda, Tina stirred and opened her eyes.

"Cassi?" she said, rubbing her eyes.

"Sorry," said Cassi. "Didn't mean to wake you."

"That's alright." Tina sat up and stretched.

"Have a nice nap?" said Cassi.

"Sure did," replied Tina. "Which is more than I can say for you. Aren't you tired?"

"Uh huh," Cassi took a long pull from her soda.

"Listen, if you're too tired to talk, get some rest. Lord knows you need it."

"No, I said I'd fill you in and I'm gonna."

Cassi finished her drink and set the empty can on the coffee table. She then told Tina of every discovery she'd made concerning the case. "I'm getting closer, Tina." She said. "Rhodes is gonna fumble the ball one time or another then I'll nail him."

"How can you be sure?" asked Tina.

"I read his file," said Cassi, removing her boots. "He's a wanna be crime boss, but doesn't have the juice or the clout to make it. Besides, most of the jobs he's done were nothing more than show off stunts to prove himself to whatever organization he's in."

"Organization?" said Tina.

"The night Mickey was killed we took in a drug cartel with a street value numbering in the millions. I've busted up a lot of drug deals, but I've never hit anything this major. It's probably the work of some sort of syndicate. That's the only conclusion I can come up with."

Tina was silent. She looked down at the carpet, thinking about what Cassi had told her. After a few minutes she said, "From what Mickey used to tell me, I know this is a dangerous game you're playing. Watch your back, Cassi...please."

"You're definitely Mickey's sister." Cassi said, grinning. "You talk like him."

The two laughed a bit then began preparing for bed. Cassi brought out a couple of sheets, a blanket, and a pillow and gave them to Tina, who fixed a place on the couch.

She then changed into a red jersey like nightshirt and white tube socks. Tina donned a pair of black lounge pants and matching sport bra. Her hair was in a ponytail style and Cassi giggled a bit.

"What's so funny?" said Tina.

"You, you kind of remind me of I Dream of Jeanie." Tina folded her arms and bowed in playful reminiscence of the popular TV character, and she and Cassi laughed again.

"By the way, Cassi, thanks for letting me stay here during my vacation," said Tina, sitting on the couch.

"No sweat," said Cassi, "What're friends for?" She turned out the lights and walked toward the bedroom.

"Cassi are you sure you can handle Rhodes?" said Tina. "I mean...he killed Mickey."

Silhouetted by the light from her bedroom, Cassi turned to face her friend. "Don't worry about it, Tina. Guys like him slip up sooner or later. Besides, he's already made one mistake."

"What's that?" asked Tina.

"He killed Mickey, and not me." Cassi replied, coldly.

Jack Rhodes angrily pounded his fist on the nightstand as he hung up the telephone. He'd just been informed that He was to stand down and Freeman would take charge of the forthcoming operation. He couldn't believe what he'd heard. How could this have happened? One minute he'd been in charge of everything, now there was nothing. Then he remembered...Freeman. He went to the kitchen and pulled a beer from the refrigerator. Opening the can, he turned it up and didn't stop drinking until the container was empty. That was it. Freeman had loused up his glory for the last time, and he'd had enough. It was time to go to work.

CHAPTER 7
THE ENIGMA

Nick Freeman and the six men with him sat down quietly in their cars, waiting for their contact to arrive. They'd been waiting at the abandoned factory for ours and some them were getting impatient and restless. But Freeman had played the "Hurry up and wait." Game countless times with his recon squad during his time in the Marines and was used to the silence and feelings of isolation that came with the job. He turned on his radio and hit the talk button, "Anybody wanting to take a leak, do it quick." Car doors opened and closed and footfalls sounded on the gravel as men went out to relieve themselves.

Before long, the sound of diesel engines broke the pre-dawn silence. Freeman and the men with him got out of their car as the others gathered around, watching four trucks lumber onto the lot. As their engines died down, Freeman walked over to the lead truck and greeted the driver. "Were you followed?" he asked.

"No," said the driver, climbing down from the cab." Everything went like clockwork."

Freeman nodded. "Good to see you're punctual."

No sooner than he spoke than bright headlights, floodlights, and flashing red and blue lights surrounded the procession. A voice boomed from a bullhorn. "Everyone stay right where you are and don't move. If you want to be blasted to pieces, by all means put up a fight and you'll get a cold slab at the morgue for your trouble. Surrender quietly and you'll get a nice, cozy cell downtown, courtesy of Captain Warden of the Santa Bella Police!"

For a moment, Freeman was astounded as he looked at the lights and heard and sounds of pistols and rifles cocking. He pulled his pistol and fired at the officers.

"Take Cover!" Warden yelled to his men. The truck drivers scattered in all directions as a furious gunfight broke out. Muzzle flashes of dozens of automatic and semi automatic weapons lighted the darkness. Bullets ripped into the ground, vehicles, and bodies. A spray of blood hit Warden as an officer next to him took a bullet in the head and fell to the ground. Sighting on a figure moving through the smoke, Warden fired his 44 automatic and brought the man down. He shot twice more at another target before a spray of automatic fire ripped into the vehicle he was using for cover, putting his head down. He yelled to his men, "Flank them and cut them off! I don't want anything getting out of here!"

As their comrades covered them, some of the officers manned their vehicles and drove down the small slope and amid a hail of bullets, formed a barrier with cars behind the diesels. Warden opened the car door and pulled a gas mask from under the seat. "Break out the gas!" he yelled, putting his mask on. He'd come prepared. Warden figured there was going to be a fight, so he had one officer keep the trunk of his car open and filled with anything they might need. One by one the officers donned their masks and Warden gave the go ahead to fire.

Freeman spotted the blockade behind the trucks and pulled a hand grenade from his car, pulled the pin and let it fly. The deadly explosive sailed over and bounced twice before rolling neatly under one of the patrol cars. Remembering his training, Freeman dropped to the ground behind his car and covered up with his weapon ready.

The policemen heard the grenade hit the ground and tried to run but too late the bomb detonated and the men were engulfed in a blistering ball of flame, glass, and metal. Freeman rose and fired several shots toward the flames to weed out any stragglers who might have survived the blast, though he doubted it. As his confederates continued to fire at the police, Freeman jumped into his car and started it up. Jerking the vehicle into gear he headed straight toward where he'd tossed the grenade at top speed and smashed his way through the flaming wreckage that had once been patrol cars.

As the CS gas canister burst among the combatants, Warden peered through the rising cloud and saw Freeman's escape attempt. Taking a deep breath he removed his mask and radioed the police station.

"This is Captain Warden at the west side factory. We need back up, an ambulance, and a fire truck."

Natasha's voice came over the radio. "Roger, understood, Captain...wait one." There was a moment of silence. "Hang on, sir...back up is coming...still working on the ambulance and fire truck."

Warden removed his mask again. "Do what you can, dispatch. Also, we've got an escape in progress. Suspect is black male wearing a business suit and driving a brown Cadillac...Los Angeles plates."

"Roger, Captain," came the answer.

In the blue-gray light of dawn, Cassi Day unlocked and got into her car. As she turned the ignition, the radio crackled. "Gunfight at west side factory...officers down...escape in progress...all available units respond." Cassi picked up the handset and hit the talk button. "5 0 6 responding," she said, and hung up the handset. Backing out of her driveway, she switched gears and roared up the street, placing a flashing blue light on her dashboard.

Freeman gunned the Cadillac through the streets. He almost wanted to laugh. Santa Bella's finest didn't know they were dealing with an ex recon marine, but they sure found out the hard way. What confused him was how those simpletons found out about the shipment. None of them ha discussed their merger abroad. Not he, Scorpio, the Asians none of them. With the others ruled out, that only left... Rhodes of course! He'd been the only other person to know about he transaction, plus who else had a better reason for wanting him out of the way? He'd no sooner put two and two together when he saw a blue Trans AM charging straight toward him on a head-on collision course. The sudden attack startled him so that he reflexively swerved to avoid the oncoming vehicle and ran into a metal lamppost.

Cassi hit the breaks and turned left. The tires squealed as her car turned broadside, creating slight blockade in the street. Pulling the key from the ignition, she jumped out of the car, jerked her Beretta from its holster, and ran toward the disabled vehicle. When she was at the least five yards from the car she pointed her weapon at the driver's window and eased forward. Nearing the car, she saw that Freeman was gone. She scanned the streets with a stricken expression, but saw only her car and a few onlookers, who'd, began to gather. Cassi ran back to her car, got in and turned her radio on P.A. "Attention all civilians," she said. "For your own safety please vacate the streets immediately. Clear this area!" Cassi got back out of the car and no sooner than she closed the door, than a gun fired and the bullet hit the street just inches from her foot. She dove over the car's hood and hit the pavement rolling, as terrified citizens screamed and ran in all directions to get out of the sniper's view. Sirens wailed and three police cruisers came rushing in.

Following Cassi's example, the officers parked their cars broadside, reinforcing the blockade. As they emerged from their cars, Cassi yelled, "Watch it!" We got a sniper!" The gun fired again and an officer clutched his chest and went down. Cassi looked around and saw something move out of the corner of her eye. It was a hand aiming a pistol from an alleyway. She jumped up from behind the car, somersaulted into the open, and fired her pistol at the area.

The morning air echoed with the sound of heavy gunfire as the other officers fired toward the alley as well. The gunman retreated and Cassi went after him. As she reached the mouth of the alley, she heard a gun being cocked and spun back around the corner before the weapon discharged, hitting an officer, who'd been coming up behind her for support. Cassi swore and dragged the wounded officer out of the line of fire, as another bullet whizzed past her head and struck the wrecked Cadillac across the street. She quickly inspected his wound. It wasn't serious. She pulled a handkerchief from her jacket and put it on his wound "Keep pressure on it." She told him.

Standing, she peered cautiously around the corner...nothing. She moved forward and took cover behind a trash compactor, her eyes scanning the alley and the rooftops. Her heart pounded. Her muscles tightened and adrenaline surged through her body, washing over her like a tidal wave. She expected to feel a hot bullet tear into her chest, blast her spine apart, and end her life at any moment, for the quarry she was after was good and not to be taken lightly. When no more shots came, she eased forward.

Suddenly a female scream came from the other side of the alley. Cassi rushed out the other side of the alley and saw Freeman pulling a small girl away from her mother. He viciously backhanded the girl's mother, knocking her against one of the buildings. The woman sank to ground unconscious, and Freeman put a gun to the crying girl's head.

"Drop it!" yelled Cassi, pointing her weapon.

"Back off!" shouted Freeman, cocking his own pistol. "Get back or I'll blow the little tramps head off right now!"

"Freeze!" someone yelled from behind Freeman. Cassi glanced past him to see four SWAT team members aiming their weapons at him. She recognized their leader as Captain William Cardigan.

"Hold your fire, Cardigan," she called. "He's got a child!" Cassi turned her attention back to Freeman. "You can't win this. Whether you go to jail or the morgue is up to you!"

"That's where you 're wrong," snapped Freeman. "If I go to the morgue, I won't go by myself!"

"What do you want?"

"I already got it, doll," said Freeman. "I got control of this situation and a way out of it." He jerked his head backward, indicating the young lady's car, the keys still in the ignition. "And just to make sure you don't get too cute, I'm taking cutie pie here along for insurance."

"She's just a child!" cried Cassi.

"You really break my heart, you know that?" Freeman replied nonchalantly. "Now drop that gun and back off. Anybody gets cute and I'll splatter her little brains all over the ground!"

Cassi glanced at the terrified girl once more then slowly lowered her pistol and set it on the ground. She kicked the weapon over to Freeman, who squatted to collect it, shifting his grip on the young girl as he did so. It was then that his tiny hostage bit him as hard as she could. Yelling in pain, Freeman dropped the child.

Cassi saw her chance and rushed in, grabbing his gun hand. "Run, honey," she said, wrestling with Freeman. "Get clear!"

Having landed on her hands and knees, the little girl got to her feet and ran into the waiting arms of one the SWAT members, who promptly got her to safety. "Go!" shouted Cardigan at another of his team members, who instantly ran forward and rescued the young girls mother, who lay stirring on the alley floor. When both hostages were safe, Cardigan and his men returned their attention to the scuffle between Cassi and Freeman.

Cassi had wrenched the pistol out of Freeman's hand kicked it out of his reach. Jerking one of her arms free, she thrust a knee up into freeman's stomach and gave him a forearm smash to the jaw. Freeman staggered backward, dragging her with him. He punched her twice in the stomach and aimed another punch at her face, only to find that the young woman was too quick. She parried the swing and head butted him in the face. Blood flowed from his nose where she'd hit him.

As they continued to wrestle, Freeman pulled her off balance, flipped her over his shoulder, and slammed her painfully onto the pavement. He tried to stomp on her, but the lithe officer rolled to the side and kicked upward, catching Freeman in the stomach. Cassi got to her feet, jumped up and did a spinning hook-kick, but Freeman ducked under and punched her hard in the ribs, knocking the wind out of her. He then gave her a backhanded strike that sent her staggering backward. Recovering quickly, the young lieutenant rushed forward, tackled him around the waist, and rammed him against one of the buildings.

" That's enough!" said Cardigan. Freeman looked and saw Cardigan's AR-15 pointed at him. The SWAT members threw Freeman against a building and frisked him, as Cassi caught her breath. She was furious.

"What the hell took you, Cardigan?" she flared. "You waiting for him to kill me?"

"I love to watch a good fight," Cardigan said, unlocking his weapon. "And you're pretty good."

"You think this is some kind of dumb game or something?"

"Hey, ease up, Day. You got your man, didn't you?"

Upon hearing her name, Freeman stiffened. Could this be the infamous Cassi Day that he'd heard of? Was she the one who'd shut down the syndicate's operations in Burbank? He glanced at the beautiful woman arguing with SWAT captain, as the troopers handcuffed him. It was hard to believe, but the way she'd fought, the tenacity, the fierceness...

"I ought to bust you right in the chops for that, Cardigan!"

"I wouldn't try it," warned Cardigan. "With your knack for getting into trouble, you can't afford any more screw ups."

"Look, your being an ex Green Beret doesn't scare me, so don't test me you trigger happy son of a..."

"That'll be enough, lieutenant." The two officers turned to see Warden emerging from the alley. "We've all got reports to file, so how about we get to it, eh?" As Cassi turned to leave, Cardigan spoke,

"I'm glad he showed up because I'd hate to have to whip your cute little butt, Day."

Cassi turned around and lunged at Cardigan, but Warden restrained her. "I said that'll be all, lieutenant!" Cassi glared at Cardigan a second longer then turned and disappeared back down the alley.

"Boy, what a hot head," said Cardigan. "I don't see how you put up with a she-devil like, her."

Straining to keep his composure, Warden turned to face the SWAT captain. "Let's get something straight, Cardigan. That she-devil, as you call her, has brought in more known felons than you and your whole team can shake a stick at. Number two, your Green Beret training and SWAT team expertise mean nothing to her, cause I've seen her crack tougher nuts than you. And number three, if it were me I'd watch what I said around her, because I might not be here to save your arrogant hide next time."

As Cassi walked to her car someone called her. "Excuse me, officer." She turned to see Freeman's ex-hostages waving to her. They started toward her but were stopped by a uniformed officer, who was trying to keep the area clear. Cassi walked up and put a hand on the man's shoulder. "It's okay," she said, and the officer stepped aside.

"Thank you for saving my daughter," said the young lady, tearfully. "She's my only..." her words trailed off into sobs and she held the little girl tightly.

Cassi gently touched the young lady's shoulder. "I'm flattered, and I wish I could take the bows, but God deserves the real credit, not me. He put me in the right place at the right time, miss..."

"Ellis, Mandy Ellis," said the young woman, wiping her tears.

"Miss Ellis." Cassi repeated. She then looked at the little girl. "And what's your name, sweetie?"

"Glenda," she said, meekly.

Cassi smiled and gently stroked Glenda's face. "You're a good girl, Glenda. And I'm sure you'll make a fine woman some day. Really, I should be thanking you."

"Me?" said Glenda.

"Uh huh, if you hadn't got the bad man's attention, I might not have been able to help." Glenda smiled.

"Officer, who are you, so we can pray for you?" said Mandy.

"I'm Cassi Day."

"Thank you again."

Cassi smiled again and waved. "Se ya' around." She walked back to her car, started it up, and drove away, leaving the two grateful females amidst onlookers and police.

CHAPTER 8

HOOK, LINE, AND SINKER

Jack Rhodes felt good as he sat on the side of his bed. Not only had he returned to DOC's strip club, but also he'd gotten Conchita, the pretty Latino stripper to accompany him back to his room. He'd wined and dined her and showed her a good time and in return she'd shown him one. He glanced back at her lying curled up in the bed and stoked her black hair. He then got up and went to the restroom to relieve himself. On his way back to bed the phone rang, and he answered. "Yeah?" he said.

"Yeah, hey, I hear you're selling snow," said a shaky, female voice.

"Who's this?" Rhodes asked, warily.

"Shauna," she said. "Look, I...I need a fix. I'll pay what ever you want and If you want me, I'm yours, but I just gotta have.... some snow, y'know?"

"Whoa, sweetheart," said Rhodes. No need to get desperate. How'd you find out about me?"

"Turk told me." Shauna stammered.

"So why didn't you just go to him?"

"He was out and didn't have any more." Shauna drew a quivering breath. "Look, if you d-don't want my money or my body, I can just..."

"Whoa, hold it," said Rhodes, urgently. "Don't be so hasty. How do I know that Turk sent you?" There was a silence on the other end and Turk's was next voice Rhodes heard.

"Hey, dude," he said. "Can you dig this little honey? She's really hard up for some stash."

"Yeah, I see," said Rhodes. "Look Turk, don't go telling people about me. It's not good for business. What if she tells somebody else?"

"Don't sweat it, " said Turk. "I know her, and she's cool. She won't say anything."

"You're sure?" Rhodes asked.

"Oh yeah. She just wants a fix, and bad."

"Okay," said Rhodes. "We'll meet at the Laundromat as usual at midnight tonight, and tell miss Shauna don't forget the cash."

"I'll bring everything you want." Shauna said, "Just bring the snow."

"You got it, doll," said Rhodes, and he hung up the phone. Conchita stirred and looked at him.

"Jack?"

"Right here, babe," he said, looking back at her.

"Is everything Okay?"

"Yeah, just a little business matter, that's all." She smiled as he got back under the covers with her and as he positioned himself on top of her, she wrapped her legs around him and gave him a kiss.

A cool spring breeze blew through the night as Rhodes' car pulled onto deserted Laundromat parking lot. Glancing up at he dimly lit building. Rhodes cut the engine and flashed his headlights twice to let Turk know he was there. In acknowledgement, Turk flashed the building's lights twice then returned them to their dim tint. Rhodes killed the headlights and got out of the car, looking around warily as he did. He then strode toward the building, carrying a brown duffle bag full of cocaine. He entered the Laundromat and was greeted heartily by Turk.

"What's going on, my man?"

"Let's just get down to business, huh?" said Rhodes, holding up one hand. "Time is money, y 'know?"

"Yeah sure, no problem, dude," Turk said. Shauna's upstairs in the office."

"What's she look like?" asked Rhodes, as they boarded the freight elevator.

"See for yourself," Turk said, closing the door. "She's something else." With a sly smile he punched the up button. Rhodes grinned as the engines whined and the elevator started upward. When they reached their destination, they disembarked and walked through the hallway to where Turk's business table was set up. Rhodes set the duffle bag on the table.

"Okay, so where is she?" he demanded.

"Be cool, man," Turk said, looking toward the sub hallway in the back. Shauna, the snowman's here."

Minutes later a shapely, black woman wearing a black bodysuit, and a black motorcycle jacket with a matching leather miniskirt emerged from the hallway. On her feet were white, ankle-length boots and her jet black hair was in a ponytail style with her bangs gently touching the dark sunglasses she wore.

"Man, you weren't kidding," said Rhodes, looking her up and down. "She's a knockout!"

The woman sauntered up to them, glanced briefly at Turk, and then nodded to Rhodes. "You got the stuff?"

Rhodes unzipped the bag, reached in and placed several clear plastic bags of coke on the table. "There you go, luscious. You got the cash?"

The young woman turned coolly around, facing the sub hallway. She snapped her fingers and instantly a stocky Latino man wearing a dark suit came forth, carrying a brief case. Holding the case horizontally, the man opened it and Rhodes' eyes popped as he gazed upon several rows of hundred dollar bills. With a sweeping gesture of her hand, the young woman indicated the money as a showgirl would a new car.

"You're welcome to all of it," she said. "And if that's not enough, you're welcome to me too." She took off her coat, revealing her hour-glass figure and with the grace of a model, advertised the magnificent specimen of womanhood she was, seductively running her hands up and down her toned thighs.

Rhodes didn't know if he were dreaming or not, but if he was he didn't want to awaken. Here he was with a case full of money and a sexy young woman, who was willing to give him her body when he wanted it. *If I just had all the free beer I could drink, I'd be in heaven!* he thought. Even the Latino girl, Conchita, didn't compare to this woman. "First thing's first," he said, getting a hold of himself. "Mind if I count the money?"

"Help yourself," said Shauna. She took the briefcase from her bodyguard and handed it to Rhodes, who moved some of the coke aside and set the case on the table.

When the count was finished Rhodes gave a low whistle. There was fifty thousand dollars in the case, which was far more than he'd expected. He expected five or maybe ten grand so he could talk her up and get more cash, but this payment totally blew him away. Satisfied, he fastened the case and stood to face his clients. "Well, I guess this concludes our little transaction. And don't worry, babe. I'll definitely take a rain check on the...other arrangement."

Shauna sat on the table and leaned back a bit, supported by her hands. She crossed her legs, giving him a great view of them. "I'll be waiting," she said, seductively.

Unable to resist, Rhodes rubbed her calves and she stiffened a bit as his hand moved up to her thighs. "A little tense, baby?" he said, his eyes roving lustfully over her toned body.

"I'm always like this when I need a hit," she said, uneasily.

Rhodes' hand went higher until his fingertips were under her skirt. The warm, smooth feel of her skin aroused him sexually and his penis began to push against the front of his pants, uncontrollably. At the last possible second, Rhodes withdrew his hand and patted her legs. "Don't worry. That stash will loosen you up." He took the briefcase and headed for the elevator. "Gotta' burn out now," he said, over his shoulder. "Catch you later, doll."

Shauna blew him a kiss as he and Turk boarded the elevator again. She sighed in relief as the doors closed and the freight descended.

The Latino man went to the window where he watched Rhodes get into his car and drive away. "Whew!" he said, looking back at her. "That was close."

Cassi Day, alias Shauna, removed her sunglasses and retrieved her jacket. "You're telling me," She said. "I swear if he'd moved his hand any higher, I'd have kicked his brains out!"

The Latino officer chuckled silently at her statement. "It could've been worse, amiga. He could've kissed you."

Cassi frowned at her friend in disgust. "You really know how to take the fun out of things don't you, Sanchez?" The Latino officer laughed again, as she spoke into the tiny microphone fastened to her brassiere. "Did you get that?"

"We got it," came Warden's reply. "You okay?"

"Nothing a week in Jamaica wouldn't fix." She said, with a chuckle.

Just then four plain clothed officers emerged from the stairwell and entered the room. "How'd it go?" Cassi asked.

"Like clockwork," said the sergeant in charge. "The homing devices are in place and well hidden. We're tracking the vehicle from the van now."

"How'd you get that equipment, Steve?" said Cassi.

"I got a buddy in the FBI who owes me favors."

Cassi grinned. "Always did like a man with connections. Okay, let's go see where that car's going." Putting on her jacket, Cassi boarded the elevator with her fellow officers, and went down to the street level. They left the building and walked across the lot to a black van, where the tall, muscular figure of Captain Warden stood waiting.

"So, that's the one who iced Mickey?" he said, as the other officers got into the van.

"Yeah, that's him." Cassi answered.

Though she'd spoken calmly, Warden saw a slight flash of anger in her eyes at the mention of Mickey and wished he'd chosen his words more carefully. "You've almost got him, lieutenant. Don't lose control." Cassi nodded. "Speaking of which, I was impressed by the way you handled yourself in there. I know this has been hard for you."

"I have my moments. " replied Cassi, grinning. Warden grinned too and followed her into the surveillance van.

The van's interior resembled a small command center, with a small desk, two rolling chairs, a monitor and rows of buttons and switches. *This isn't a van it's a spaceship*, Cassi thought, as she glanced around at the vehicle's interior.

"We got him," said a female officer. Cassi moved over to the monitor and watched closely as the blip that was Rhodes' car moved across the screen.

Days later a police van lumbered through the streets, carrying Freeman to court. He'd made his one phone call, and wasn't at all surprised when no one answered. He grinned ruefully as he remembered a statement he'd signed as a marine. If you're captured, or if any information leaks, the U.S. will deny any participation, or even knowledge of your existence. His situation would seem ironic to any one else, but he'd expected no less when the syndicate took him in. He was as expendable now as he'd been in the Marines.

Suddenly he heard horns blasting and tires screeching outside. The van swerved violently from side to side and the panic-stricken driver struggled to control the vehicle. When the officer guarding him glanced toward the cab, Freeman attacked. Throwing himself onto the startled officer, he grabbed the CAR-15 in the man's hands and head butted him in the face, stunning him. Freeman then snatched the weapon from the officer and smashed the stock into the man's temple, knocking him to the floor. The ex marine then chambered a round and put a bullet through the back of the downed officer's head, sending a spray of blood, brains, and bone fragments all over the floor and walls.

Something rammed violently against the side of the van, forcing it off the road, and the driver screamed as the vehicle hit the side of a building. Freeman then heard tires screech to a halt, car doors slam, and the sound of running feet and weapons being cocked. Before the dazed driver and his escort could react, they were shot at point-blank range with silenced weapons. Freeman pointed his weapon as someone shot off the locks and opened the van's back doors. Two men stood out side holding automatic weapons. "Let's go!" said one of the men, waving Freeman forward.

Rhodes happily ran his fingers through the money he'd made from the sale. It had been the biggest haul he'd made since he'd been with the syndicate. It was too bad that the syndicate supplied him with the drugs he needed for selling, otherwise he'd have his own organization. Then he thought, *Why contend for a position you may never get when you could make a little money on the side?* Scorpio had several warehouses Rhodes could "borrow" coke from and sell at whatever price he chose. Then he could enjoy the best of everything, like his boss. The best cars, women, foods, anything he wanted. And he could do it secretly from his hotel room and never once worry about escaping the syndicate. The more he thought about it, the more intrigued he became. He was sure he could make it happen. And even better, Freeman was out of his way as well. Rhodes felt so good he decided to go celebrate. Pushing the brief case under his bed, he straightened his clothes combed his hair and left the room, locking the door behind him.

Flanked by the two men who'd rescued him, Freeman silently rode the elevator toward its destination, anger eating away at him like cancer. When the elevator reached the top floor, the trio exited and walked down the carpeted hallway to Scorpio's office. One of the escorts knocked on the door. "Enter." came the answer from inside. The man stepped aside and Freeman opened the door and walked into the room, where Scorpio stood waiting, his hands clasped behind his back.

"Ah, good to see you're still in one piece, Mister Freeman," he said, his voice as icy as ever. "I know what happened and I know you're not to blame. But I want to see if we're on the same wavelength."

"Rhodes, sir," said Freemen. "It's got to be him. No one else has the motive."

"I concur, " Scorpio said. The syndicate boss walked back to his desk and turned to face his enforcer. "He's becoming more trouble than he's worth. You don't need my permission to deal with this matter." A dangerous smile crossed Freeman's face, as he mentally made plans for Rhodes' demise. Then Scorpio's voice broke his chain of thought. "Is there something else troubling you, mister Freeman, detective Day perhaps?"

"Yes, sir." Freeman answered, sullenly.

"Yes, my sources tell me you had quite a run-in with her."

The rage that had been eating Freeman slowly came to a sudden boil. "The next time we meet, she's as good as dead!"

"In due time, Mister Freeman," Scorpio assured, calmly. "First let's attend to the matter at hand...Jack Rhodes.

CHAPTER 9
DEADLY GAME

Cassi saw several police cruisers and an ambulance surrounding a crash site and pulled her car out of traffic to investigate. Parking behind one of the cruisers, she got out and walked toward the site, which was surrounded by police tape marked, POLICE LINE DO NOT CROSS. As she neared the tape, one of the uniformed officers came over to stop her, but Cassi showed him her ID and badge and he stepped aside, holding the tape up for her to walk under.

Recognizing a few of the officers, she went over to where they were huddled around a stretcher. "Hey guys, what's up?"

"Cassi, are we glad to see you," said one of the younger officers.

"What's going on?" said Cassi.

One of the other officers reached down and pulled back the covers on the stretcher to reveal one of the downed officers who'd ridden in the van. There was a hole in his left temple but the back of his head on the right side was blown away.

The officer replaced the sheet and pointed to another stretcher. "We got another over there, same pattern. The one in the ambulance got a bullet through the back of his head. If we hadn't seen his nametag, we wouldn't know who he was. His face is gone."

Cassi's eyes narrowed in thought as she listened to the officers. Just then her radio buzzed to life, and she went back to her car. She leaned through the window and grabbed the handset. "506," she said, leaning against the car.

"Lieutenant, this is Warden," came the reply.

"Go ahead, cap."

"We ran a make on the guy you tangled with a few days ago. His name's Nick Freeman and he's an ex marine, force recon."

"Force recon, what's that?"

"Marine special forces."

"Is that right?" Cassi said, almost nonchalantly. "Anything else?"

"We can't tie him to anything but drug trafficking, but even worse...he's escaped."

"What?"

"That's right, lieutenant," confirmed Warden. "The crash site where you are now, those dead officers, all his handiwork."

Cassi angrily pounded her fist on top of her car. She stood there trying to gather her thoughts, when Warden spoke again.

"C'mon back to the station, lieutenant. We need to talk." Cassi was silent for a moment then she thumbed her handset. "I'm on my way."

"I don't get it," said Cassi, pacing back and forth in Warden's office, her hands on her hips. "How the heck did this happen?"

"It's obvious Freeman had help," said Warden.

"Any idea who?" said Cassi, still pacing.

"None," answered Warden, shaking his head. "From what we've gathered from a few witnesses some other vehicle came from nowhere, tangled with the van, and ran it off the road."

Cassi stopped pacing stroked her chin thoughtfully. "Scorpio must value him a lot to bust him out that quick."

Warden looked at her. "You think that's who he's working for?"

"I don't know, but it makes sense. We already know Rhodes is mixed up in drug trafficking, and now we catch Freeman doing the same thing. For all I know, this may be two different things altogether. But somehow I don't think so. They may be in this together, but I can't prove anything just yet."

Warden thought about what she'd said for a moment then nodded. "Well, I've already put out an APB on Freeman. Something's bound to turn up somewhere. You going on with your original plan?"

"Yeah, I'm going after Rhodes tonight."

"All right," said Warden. "I'll get you some back up."

"No!" Cassi said, abruptly. "With all due respect sir, Rhodes is mine."

"Lieutenant, we've been through this before. This isn't Dodge City and you're not Matt Dillon."

"I'm not trying to be," said Cassi, folding her arms. "But it was my partner he killed. I want to bring him in."

"Not without back up!" Warden said, firmly. "You think I don't know what it's like to lose a partner, detective? I lost eight men before I made captain, eight good men. I felt the same then as you do now. I wanted to get all the bad guys too. But it takes more than courage. You're gonna need help sometimes."

Cassi unfolded her arms and put her hands on her hips again, her eyes locked on Warden's. "Well, we're not gonna bring him in, standing here talking about it either."

"We either do it by the book or not all."

Cassi gave Warden an incredulous look and swallowed a sudden lump in her throat. "You can't be serious, captain. You told me Mickey was like a son to you and now you want to withdraw your support, just like that?"

Warden stood. "He was like as son to me, but my duty as police officer comes before personal feelings. Have you been on the streets so long that you've forgotten the rules of conduct?"

"No, sir, But I have been on them long enough to know what will work," Cassi said. "Look captain, I know you don't always go along with what I do out there, but even you gotta admit I get the job done. If I screw up you can have my shield, my job, even my head on a silver platter if you want it, but until then, give me my shot."

Warden silently stared at Cassi for several minutes, contemplating what she'd said and wondering what to do with this young, headstrong woman in front of him. "All right, lieutenant," he said, jabbing a finger at her. "You got one shot and you'd better make it good."

"Thanks cap," Cassi said, as she turned to leave. "I owe you one."

"You owe me too many." Warden said.

Cassi sat in her car on the parking lot of the Holiday Inn where Rhodes resided, listening to her radio, which was turned down. She took a sip of 7up and leaned back, listening to a song by Genesis entitled "That's all", her eyes never leaving the hotel. She was tired.

She'd been on dozens of stakeouts before, but Mickey had always been with her, keeping watch while she grabbed a few winks of sleep. But now she was going solo and had to keep her guard up. She didn't want Mickey's killer slipping past her, especially after all she'd been through to get this close.

The song ended and Cassi had just begun chewing a stick of gum when a car drove onto the lot, pulled over and cut its engines and lights. She waited a few minutes but no one emerged from the car, and it had tinted windows, so she couldn't see who was in it. This made her uneasy, and every nerve in her body was alerted. Her muscles tightened as adrenaline pumped through her and her heartbeat quickened. For a moment she thought her imagination was running away with her, but the sixth sense she'd developed on the streets had kicked in too many times for her to dismiss this as pure coincidence. She couldn't put her finger on it, but something just wasn't right.

Just then Rhodes came out of the hotel and began walking toward his car. Cassi put on her shades, turned on the tiny tape recorder in her jeans pocket and got out of her car, walking silently toward him.

She was about three yards from him when the dark vehicle started up and drove straight for them. Cassi heard its tires screeching as it came and she and Rhodes spared a glance at the oncoming vehicle. Cassi ran forward, tackled Rhodes around the waist, and rolled him over the hood of the car. They hit the pavement on the other side just as the mysterious vehicle rammed hard into Rhodes' car. Rhodes started to look up but Cassi shoved his head back to the pavement.

"You'd better keep your head down unless you want it shot off!" She warned.

As if to punctuate her statement, a stuttering burst of automatic fire exploded through the night. Bullets ripped through the car's windows and smacked into the concrete wall on the other side of the car, and Cassi covered her head and face, as shards broken glass rained down on her and Rhodes.

Jerking her pistol from its holster, Cassi somersaulted backward into the open, rolled to her knees, and came up firing. Her sudden attack caught the startled gunman off guard and before he knew what had happened, one of Cassi's bullets caught him in the forehead, knocking him over the back of the dark Cadillac.

The driver backed the car away then roared toward the parking lot exit. Cassi fired again and blew out the back windshield of the receding vehicle, which continued on out of the lot. The hotel manager and several security officers came running from the entrance, as Cassi slowly stood and holstered her weapon. "What going on here?" he demanded.

Cassi unclipped her badge from her belt and showed it to him, careful not to let Rhodes see it. "Call an ambulance," she said. The manager and his men stared at the dead body and she began to get irritated "You deaf?"

The manager sent one of his guards to make the call then posted the others around the scene so none of the hotel's residents or curious bystanders would interfere.

"I don't know who you are miss, but I'm glad you were around." Rhodes said, standing up.

Cassi turned to face him. Her voice was cold and hard. "You'd better decide later whether seeing me tonight was a pleasure or not, Jack Rhodes."

Her words startled him. He stared nervously at the darkly clad female in front of him. How could this woman know his name and where to find him? Then a horrifying realization hit him like a ton of bricks...The Syndicate. Too late, Rhodes remembered Scorpio had eyes and ears everywhere. Someone must have overheard his anonymous phone call to the police in regards to the opium shipment at the factory. Scorpio found out and sent an assassin to kill him. He began to sweat and his breath came in short, nervous gasps as he tried to talk.

"L-Listen. Whatever Scorpio's paying you, I-I'll double it."

Cassi's eyes widened a bit at the mention of Scorpio's name. Obviously the man had more connections than she knew of. She decided to play a hunch. Keeping her eyes on him, she said, "Keep talking."

"S-Sure." Rhodes continued. "How much is he paying you?" Cassi chose the amount carefully.

"Ten grand."

"Hah!" said Rhodes. "I'll pay you twenty-five."

"Okay," she said. "Lead the way, and no funny business. I can still finish the job I was sent to do."

"Y-yeah, sure," stammered Rhodes.

He led her through the lobby to an elevator, which they rode silently to the floor his room was on. When they reached his place, he unlocked the door and turned on the light. Keeping her eyes on him, Cassi followed him inside and closed the door behind her. She kept one hand on her pistol, tucked into her waistband behind her, as Rhodes and pulled something from under his bed. It was a briefcase. She stepped back a safe distance as Rhodes counted out the payment. When he finished he stood and handed her the money and she pretended to count it.

"You said you'd double Scorpio's payment," she said. "What's the extra five for?" "I want you to knock off somebody for me."

"Who?"

"Well, I don't know if he's still in the Syndicate, but his name is Freeman, Nick Freeman."

Cassi's eyes narrowed slightly behind her shades. "What does he look like?"

Rhodes gave her a complete description of Freeman and her suspicious were quickly confirmed. It was the same man she'd tangled with the streets that day, and who'd murdered her fellow officers. The puzzle was now complete. There was indeed a Syndicate as she'd suspected, and a powerful one at that. But now there were two feuding factions, which had created a dissension in the ranks. Cassi remembered a bible verse saying, "A house divided against itself cannot stand." And that was exactly what was happening here. She almost laughed in spite of herself at the truth of the verse.

"I want it to look like an accident," Rhodes continued. "I can't be connected to this in any way."

"Don't worry," said Cassi, coolly. "I don't leave loose ends. But there's something else I want to know."

"What's that?" said Rhodes.

"You said a moment ago you weren't sure if Freeman was still in the Syndicate. Why wouldn't he be?"

Rhodes eyed her suspiciously. "What are you an assassin or a reporter?"

Cassi stuffed the money into her jacket. "I make it my business to know the backgrounds of all my targets, as well as the people who hire me to kill them," she said. "Just like I know you're called Fresno Jack because of the jobs you've done out there. I also know you killed a cop last month named Mick Colton during a warehouse raid, in which the police took in a large shipment of coke."

Rhodes was stunned. This woman had just told him of his past and he'd never met her; however there was something vaguely familiar about her that he couldn't quite put his finger on. Trying to regain his composure, he said, "Look, I was just trying to get outta' there. And that cop I killed wasn't my original target. He just got in the way, that's all."

Cassi nodded and turned away from him, turning off the recorder. "I see. Well, in that case I'll do my job. Jack Rhodes, you're under arrest for murder and drug trafficking."

Rhodes was taken aback. "What is this some kind of joke?" Cassi removed her sunglasses. Fear flooded Rhodes' body, paralyzing him as he looked into the blazing brown eyes glaring at him.

"Y-you!" he stammered, remembering the look in her eyes the night she'd shot him. It was a look of pure hatred. That same smoldering look was searing through his eyes and into his soul, now. Adrenaline, born from fear, surged through him and he gave Cassi a hard shove to one side and broke for the door.

But Cassi regained her balance quickly and lunged for him. His hand was already on the knob but before he could turn it, she grabbed his jacket collar from behind and jerked hard, pulling him backward. She stuck out her leg, tripping him and he fell on his back, hard. Cassi then locked the door as Rhodes, still on his back, crawled backward away from her. Turning to face him, she said, "You can either go straight to prison or you can go to the hospital and then to prison. But either way you're coming with me!"

Rhodes got to his feet and swung a right cross, at her, but Cassi blocked the swing, punched him hard in the stomach, then flipped him over her shoulder, dumping him once again on his back. "Give it up, Rhodes. It's all over," she said.

Rhodes tried to go for the door again, but Cassi grabbed him again and jerked him back. Still on the floor, he half somersaulted backward and kicked her in the head, stunning her. He quickly jumped to his feet, tackled her around the waist, and rammed her into the wall. He punched her three times in the stomach, and then lifted her off the floor in a bear hug. "I'm not going to jail!" he said, carrying her toward the balcony.

Cassi looked back and saw he was going to throw her over the side. Drawing back both hands, she slapped him so hard across both ears that the concussion burst both his eardrums. Howling with pain, Rhodes dropped her to the floor and reeled backward, holding his ears. Cassi was on her knees gasping for breath and holding her stomach where Rhodes had hit her. She looked up at him and for a split second, the memory of Mick dying in the hospital flashed through her mind. Enraged, Cassi jumped to her feet and did a spinning crescent kick, which caught Rhodes squarely in the face, knocking him backward over the coffee table. He hit the floor on his back and before he could recover, Cassi straddled him, firing lefts and rights into his face.

She was no longer thinking rationally. A red haze covered her vision and she lost every emotion except her hate, as she savagely pummeled her partner's killer. She was so far gone that she didn't hear the police pounding on the door, and barely noticed when they kicked the door in. One of the officers tackled her and rolled her off Rhodes' inert form, while another officer checked the syndicate member for life signs. "He's alive," she said. "But just barely."

Struggling in the grip of the officer who held her, Cassi let out a feral scream of rage and grief that chilled everyone in the room. She was possessed by the desire to avenge her fallen partner, and it seemed as if nothing could bring her out of the trance she was in. She'd nearly broken free of the restraining officer, when Matthew Warden rushed into the room. He stepped quickly over to Cassi and grabbed her by the shoulders, shaking her. "Lieutenant, it's me...Warden!" But Cassi continued to struggle and scream unearthly.

Warden was startled. Her screams reminded him of the possessed little girl in the Exorcist movie he'd seen when he was younger. He'd never heard her utter such a sound. He shook her even harder. "Blast it, lieutenant...look at me now!" He then slapped her hard across the cheek. Suddenly the red haze faded from her eyes and was replace by the concerned countenance of captain Warden. He was looking at her as a father would his daughter, just waking her up from a terrible nightmare. Breathing heavily, she looked at her surroundings, her eyes blinking rapidly.

Warden gently pushed her hair back out of her face. "It's over, Cassi. You got him." He said, calmly.

Dazed, she blinked at Warden a moment then looked past him at Rhodes as the other officers handcuffed him. There was very little of him that she recognized, for she'd beat him so, that his face was a swollen, bloody mass of bruises. And his legs kept buckling under him, threatening to drop him to the floor at any minute. She looked back into Warden's eyes and he sensed what was coming.

Turning his head quickly he barked an order to the other officers. "Get that sewage out of here!" The officers hastily complied with their captain's command and dragged Rhodes' swaggering form out of the room and down the hall, leaving the two of them alone. When Warden looked back at Cassi, tears were streaming down her cheeks. She opened her mouth to speak, but her throat contracted painfully and she couldn't say a word. "It's all right, Cassi," said Warden. "You've held it in too long. It's time to let go now. Let it go."

Unable to control herself any longer, Cassi Day sat on the bed and broke down and cried for the first time since she could remember, as Warden sat beside her and put an arm across her shoulders. She began to tremble all over with a sudden unexplainable chill. Warden held her close as quiet sobs shook her already trembling body. Locked in a father-daughter embrace, the two held each other until Cassi could cry no more.

CHAPTER 10
THE MESSAGE

Side by side, lieutenant Day and captain Warden disembarked the hotel elevators and walked through the lobby toward the entrance. Cassi looked at Warden and said, " I thought you weren't sending any back up."

" It's a good thing I did, or you'd have killed him," said Warden. "Am I right?"

"I didn't think it would go that far," said Cassi; remorsefully "I thought I could handle it."

"Don't sweat it, Lieutenant. I've been there before," Warden admitted. "I made the same mistake myself once."

Cassi gave him a quizzical look. "You?"

"Yup."

"What happened?"

"Review board, suspension, plus I got busted down to collecting empty shell casings on the firing range for about a year. I barely managed to stop myself before the mistake was made."

"Thanks for looking out for me." Cassi said, earnestly.

"What are friends for?" Warden said, with a chuckle.

"Oh captain, this is for you. It's Rhodes' confession." She said, handing him the miniature recorder. Warden put the recorder in his jacket pocket. "You did a good job, lieutenant"

With the help of the police, security officers were holding complaining tenants and reporters at bay near the entrance. Stopping halfway from the doors, Warden turned to Cassi. "Try to find a back exit or something. I'll handle this." Cassi nodded wearily and did as Warden said while the police captain, glimpsing the exit she was heading for, radioed for an officer to meet her there and escort her to her car. Warden then walked out the doors and into the throng of flashing camera lights, microphones, and policemen.

Cassi had no sooner closed the exit door behind her, than a blonde, female officer named Vanessa Roberts approached her. Like Cassi, she was slender and had good muscle tone from years of working out, but there was a nervous look in her eyes and Cassi knew right away that she was a rookie.

"This way, lieutenant," she said. "I'm the officer Captain Warden sent to escort you."

"How'd you know my rank?" Cassi asked, suspiciously. "How'd you even know what I look like?"

"Captain Warden gave me the info." Vanessa said, startled.

Cassi took a deep breath and slowly exhaled. She was suddenly angry with herself for not thinking that Warden could pass on information to the young lady in front of her, especially since she was a rookie. She relaxed a bit. "I'm sorry, she said. "But it's been a long night."

"So I gather," said Vanessa. "C'mon, lets get you to your car."

As they walked to her car, Cassi looked at Vanessa and said, "So, how long you been on the force?"

"To tell you the truth, I just started last week." Vanessa said, honestly.

"Really?" said Cassi. "Well, I got the feeling you'll make a pretty good cop."

"You really think so?"

"Sure, why not? You can make it like anybody else."

"Thanks for believing in me."

"Doesn't matter what I or anybody else believes," Cassi said. "It's what you believe that counts."

Vanessa smiled and nodded her understanding. "By the way, I'm Vanessa Roberts." She said, extending her hand.

Cassi shook hands with her. "I'm Cassi Day."

Vanessa's eyes widened. "Cassi Day? *The* Cassi Day?"

"That's me."

"Whoa, this is intense," said Vanessa, incredulously.

"What?" asked Cassi.

"I'm walking with a living legend. I've heard a lot about you from different officers."

"Well, people have a way of exaggerating things," said Cassi. "But underneath it all I'm a human made out of flesh, blood, and bones like you. I'm no hero, I just do my job."

They were nearly to Cassi's car when they saw two officers bringing Rhodes to a squad car. They were just about to put him in the car when Rhodes began a scuffle with them. Drawing back, he elbowed the male officer in the stomach and shoved him aside, yanking his pistol from its holster as he did so.

The female officer grabbed for her pistol, but Rhodes put a bullet into her shoulder before she could even clear her holster. She fell to the ground moaning and clutching the bleeding wound in her arm.

"C'mon!" Cassi yelled, nudging Vanessa with her elbow. Guns drawn, the two officers raced toward the fracas. "Drop it, Rhodes!" shouted Cassi, pointing her weapon.

Vanessa knelt beside her and pointed her own pistol. "You heard her." She cocked the trigger. "Nice and easy, now."

Still swaying unsteadily as a result of the beating he'd taken, Rhodes turned slowly around with his hands raised, as if to comply. "I'm not going to jail!" he said, then pointed the pistol and fired.

As the bullet whistled between them, Vanessa dove to one side and rolled firing back. But Cassi stood stock-still and fired two shots, both of which struck home. Rhodes pitched backward as one bullet hit him in the chest and the other, caught him in the forehead. He was dead before he hit the ground.

Slowly lowering her weapon, Cassi looked over at Vanessa, who was getting to her feet. "You okay?"

"Yeah, I'm okay," she said, picking up her cap. "How about you?"

"I'm all right."

Paramedics, Police officers, and reporters began running toward the scene and Cassi turned to Vanessa. "Tell the other officers to admit Paramedics only. Don't let those reporters get in here."

"Got it," said Vanessa.

As the blonde officer jogged off toward the oncoming crowd, Cassi smiled and whispered, "Oh yeah, you'll make a real good cop."

Freeman stood at he edge of the dark alley waiting from Scorpio's car to show. It wasn't long before the syndicate boss' vehicle came into view, pulled over, and flashed its headlights twice. Walking briskly toward the limousine, he circled around to the passenger side and bent down as Scorpio's window slid down electronically. "Rhodes is dead, sir," he said.

"But not by our hands it seems," said Scorpio.

"No, sir, we were about to nail him when Cassi Day interfered. She caught him and the cops were trying to take him away, when he took one of their weapons and tried to escape. Day dropped him with two shots.

"Indeed," said Scorpio, thoughtfully." He died more bravely than I thought.

"Either that or he was too afraid of a prison term."

"Nevertheless, he's out of the way." Scorpio stated, nonchalantly.

"Yes sir, but if Day was on to Rhodes, she's on to us."

"Then monitor her day and night," said Scorpio, his voice colder than Freeman had ever heard it. "Let me know what you find out, but no one touches her until I give the word."

"Understood, sir." And with that Scorpio's window glass closed and Freeman stepped back as the limousine drove up the street and disappeared from view. Walking back to his car, Freeman started it and drove off in the opposite direction.

Even with his hands cuffed, Turk slept soundly as he rode in the back seat of an unmarked police vehicle on his way to a witness protection agency. Since his involvement in her undercover operation, Cassi had him placed in protective custody until the case could be closed. The car drove silently through the night until it reached the airport.

"Hey you, with the face," said the officer driving. "Get up."

Turk groggily sat up, rubbed his eyes and followed a second officer, who'd been riding beside him out of the car. Side by side they walked through the airport, ignoring the curious glances of some of the workers and passengers, most of who were looking at he handcuffs around Turks wrists. On they walked until they reached terminal eight, where a pair of U.S. Marshals awaited them.

"Thank you, gentlemen," said one of the federal officials as his partner reached for Turk. "We'll take it from here."

"Don't let him get away from you, now." One of the policemen joked, waving to them. "The marshals waved back and took Turk toward customs. Once through there, they walked down a long, wide corridor filled with gift shops, bookstores, newsstands, and barbershops. Just when Turk thought the walking would never end, he found himself approaching a set of double doors leading not to an airplane, but an underground parking lot. He was suspicious.

"What's going on?" he said. "I thought we were taking a plane.

"There's been a change of plan," said one of the marshals. "Whoever's looking for you might anticipate your being flown out, so we're driving you." The answer seemed to satisfy Turk, and he asked no more questions. They exited the airport and walked an eighth of the way down one row of cars until they came to a gray Oldsmobile and got in.

As they drove out of the parking lot, the marshal sitting next to Turk in the back seat adjusted a ring on his left hand and a small, sharp needle protruded from it, facing his palm. Turk twisted in the seat to watch a pretty brunette girl in shorts walking down the sidewalk and the marshal tapped him lightly across the neck, driving the needle into the nerve in his spine.

Turk flinched and looked at the marshal, holding his neck. "H-hey, what did you do to me?" His vision blurred and he began to feel drowsy. He shook his head from side to side and blinked his eyes rapidly, but the more he struggled weaker he became. He looked at the marshal once more. "What d-did you..." Turk's eyes rolled back into their sockets, his eyelids closed and he slumped over.

The marshal checked Turk for a pulse and got nothing. He then put a hand under the man's nose but felt no air to indicate that he was breathing. "He's had it." He said, looking up at his partner. The driver glanced in the rearview mirror at his sidekick and nodded. The men drove around the airport twice and reentered the parking lot. Parking the car in a different space, the men discarded their "marshal" ID's inside the car then got out and disappeared into the crowd, leaving the dead man behind.

"You got him?" that's great, Cassi," said Tina as she sat on the couch across from her friend. "I wish I could've been with you."

"No you don't," Cassi said, drying her hair, having just come from the shower. "It got ugly there for a while."

"What happened?"

"He tried to shoot his way out of there before we could take him in. I just happened to be the one who dropped him."

"You did what you had to do, Cassi," said Tina.

"Something's bugging me, though."

"What's that?"

"I keep hearing the name Scorpio. Rhodes worked for him and so did another guy I had a run-in with, named Freeman. They're all part of some kind of crime syndicate and Scorpio is the head."

"How'd you come up with all this?" asked Tina.

"Well, when I busted Turk he confessed that Scorpio was his drug supplier, and later Rhodes mentioned him too," said Cassi.

"And how'd you get him to do that?"

"Get this, he thought Scorpio hired me to ice him."

"Say what?" said Tina, trying not to laugh. "You mean he thought you were some sort of hit person?"

"Can you believe that? He even paid me to knock off Freeman just so I wouldn't kill him."

"Oh no!" Unable to control herself, Tina Colton burst into hysterical laughter and laughed until she cried. Ordinarily, Cassi wouldn't laugh about the incident, but watching her friend her friend made her giggle a bit too. She would've mentioned that the money Rhodes was using was phony but Tina was laughing enough as it was. When the laughter was finished both ladies returned to business.

"So what about this Freeman guy?" said Tina.

"He's a real enigma, I'll say that for him," said Cassi. "I don't know what role he's playing in all this, but he and Rhodes were at odds with each other for some reason. Cassi put down the towel she'd been using to dry her hair, and continued, "We'd had Freeman in custody, but he escaped on his way to trial."

Tina's jaw dropped. "Are you serious?"

Cassi nodded in affirmation. " Scorpio broke him out somehow."

"What are you going to do now? said Tina.

"The captain's already put out an APB on Freeman," said Cassi combing her hair. "Like I said, I've had a run in with him before and he's not somebody you want to take lightly. Somehow I got the feeling I'm gonna run into him again, because he doesn't seem like to type who'll lay low for very long."

Tina swallowed a lump in her throat and she felt a shiver of fear go up her spine. She and Cassi had been friends for years and according to Mick's letters and phone conversations, Cassi could more than hold her own in any kind of conflict. But even though she wasn't a cop, Tina sensed something totally sinister about this syndicate that went beyond drugs...she didn't know how right she was.

The next morning as she drove to work. Cassi got a call on her radio. "5 0 6," she said into the handset.

"Roger 5 0 6,"came the answer. "There's been a triple homicide at the airport. The captain wants you to check it out."

"I'm on my way," Cassi answered. Placing the blue flashing light on her dashboard, she hit the accelerator and roared down the street, swerving into different lanes and passing the other cars like a shot. Tires squealed as Cassi's Trans AM pulled out of traffic and into the airport parking lot. Parking next to the two police cruisers outside, she cut the engine jumped out of the vehicle, and walked briskly through the airport until she came to the crime scene. Officer Steve Jansen waved to her as she made her way through the crowd of onlookers. As Cassi neared the police tape, Jansen came over and let her through.

"Hey, Steve," she said. "What's going on?"

"It's weird, Cassi. We got two U.S. Marshals here, and another stiff out in the underground area."

"Let's have a look," said Cassi, her hands on her hips. She followed Jansen over to one of the two ambulance gurneys, where the officer pulled back the covers. The man had been shot at point-blank range in the forehead and so had his partner. Cassi's eyes narrowed as she mentally analyzed the situation.

"Any ID's on these guys?"

"Yeah," said Jansen, pulling a small, clear plastic bag from his jacket. He handed it to Cassi. "Here you go."

Without removing them from the bag, she quickly inspected the ID's and they matched the men lying before her, but she wasn't satisfied. Handing them back to Jansen, she said, "Who found the bodies?"

Jansen looked around. "Uh...that janitor over there." He said, pointing to her left.

Cassi looked toward the janitor, dressed in blue coveralls and talking to a tall, heavyset, balding man in a brown suit and a gray trench coat. *Charles Hopper, just what I need*, she thought, remembering his arrogance. She and Jansen walked over and Hopper turned to face them.

"Well, well," he said, sarcastically. "Cassi Day, what brings you out here this morning?"

"Same thing that brings you." Cassi answered.

"Yeah, well I got things under control here," Hopper said, with a smirk. "Not much going on here for a loose cannon like you."

Trying to keep her composure, Cassi folded her arms and locked eyes with Hopper. "Look detective, I was called in here to check this out and that's what I'm gonna do. I'm sure you won't mind if I look around a bit."

"Help yourself," said Hopper, grudgingly. "But you won't find any more than we did."

Cassi sneered in disgust, as the burly detective stalked angrily away. She looked at Jansen." How do you stay partnered with that jerk?"

"Believe me, Cassi, it's not easy," said Jansen, rolling his eyes.

Cassi grinned and patted her friend on the back. "Talk to this young man and find out where he found those bodies. I'm going downstairs."

"All right," said Jansen.

Cassi walked down to the underground parking area, where paramedics were wheeling another gurney toward the ambulance. "Hold up a minute, gentlemen," she said, holding up her badge. The men stopped their work as she approached and pulled back the sheet to reveal Turk's body. Cassi closed her eyes and her heart cringed. *You just couldn't leave those drugs alone, could you?* she thought, sadly. *Why didn't you come to me? I would've helped you.* Then she noticed what looked like a piece of paper just barely sticking out from under his shirt. She reached in and pulled out a small envelope which read 'To Cassi Day.' "Where was this body found?" she asked the lead medic.

"In that car over there," He said pointing to a gray Oldsmobile surrounded by police tape and guarded by two uniformed officers.

Cassi looked to where he was pointing and nodded. "Okay, thanks a lot guys. You can take off now." As soon as the ambulance was gone, Cassi opened the envelope and pulled out a note, which read, 'Don't screw around with the syndicate.' She put the note back inside the envelope and stuffed the envelope in her jacket pocket. She then went over to the officers and asked if any of them had talked to the one who'd found the body. Neither of them had, so she went back upstairs to talk to Jansen.

Later that morning Cassi walked into Warden's office and gave him a quick briefing on the airport situation. "One of the homicide victims was Turk."

"Turk? You mean the junkie you caught?" said Warden, looking up at her from his desk.

"Yeah," she reached into her jacket and pulled the note from the inside pocket and handed it to her captain. "I found this on him."

Warden read the note then laid it on his desk. "Did you find out anything else?"

"No, I'm waiting for an autopsy report from the coroner."

"All right," said Warden. "Keep me posted."

"Right," Cassi said. She turned to go, but just as her hand touched the doorknob, Warden called to her.

"Oh lieutenant, I almost forgot." He reached into his desk and pulled out a small business card and handed it to her. "Found this on Rhodes' body that night."

Cassi examined the card. It read Techno Computer Company. "I've heard of this company before. They sell a lot of name brand computers," she said, her eyes narrowing in thought. "In fact, a friend of mine, who recently bought one from them, said their main branch is in L.A. But they have a smaller branch right here in northwest Santa Bella."

As she glanced once more at the card, Warden saw a familiar gleam in her eyes and knew what she was thinking.

"Lieutenant, don't go out there stepping on any toes." He warned.

Cassi looked up at him and chuckled a bit. "Don't worry, cap," She said, putting the card in her jeans pocket. "I've got tons of other things to do." She thanked Warden for the card, opened the door, and closed it behind her as she left. On her way back to her desk she thought, *Besides, I don't step on toes, Captain. I bust heads!*

CHAPTER 11

THE FEDS

Cassi had no sooner finished writing her report on the airport homicide than her phone rang. "Detective Day," she said into the receiver.

"Ah, good afternoon, detective. This is Doctor Rogers from the Coroner's office, hope I haven't caught you at a bad time."

"No, not at all," she said. "What'd you find out, Doc?"

"The young man you called Turk died of a lethal injection."

"What?" said Cassi, astonished.

"Yes, there's a small puncture wound in the back of his neck and we found a huge amount of poison in his blood when we took a sample of it, thought you might want to take a look."

"You bet I would," said Cassi. "I'll be there as soon as I can. Thanks for calling, doc." She hung up the phone and then took her report to Warden. "Turk was poisoned. The doc found a puncture wound in his neck. I'm going down there to verify the situation. If, that is, nothing else came up for me."

"No, nothing new, lieutenant. Take off."

"Thanks, Cap," said Cassi. And with that, she turned and disappeared through the main area and down the hall.

Freeman and another man watched Cassi's house from a car, parked just down the street. They'd only been there an hour when Tina Colton, clad in a black, sleeveless tee shirt, faded blue shorts, and white sneakers, came down the driveway, carrying a bag of trash. She left the trash bag at the edge of the driveway and walked back up to the house as a garbage truck lumbered down the street toward the house. Freeman adjusted his binoculars and looked again, just as Tina turned to watch the men pick up the trash.

"Well well," he said. "What have we here?"

"What do ya' see?" said he other man, eagerly. "Looks like miss Day has company, pretty company at that. That just may be a bit of insurance as well." Freeman put down the binoculars and picked up a car phone. Dialing a private number, he waited as the phone rang. Suddenly someone picked up.

"Report," said Scorpio.

"Boss, I think you're gonna like this."

Cassi Day stood with Dr. Rogers discussing the fallen figure lying on the table between them. Turk's body had been positioned to where it was lying on its stomach and the doctor had moved the man's long hair to the side exposing his neck. "As I stated earlier, lieutenant, here's the puncture wound and it's right at the base of the skull, where the poison was injected," said the doctor, using an index finger to indicate the puncture.

Cassi leaned forward and briefly examined the wound then her eyes turned to Rogers. "Any idea what kind of poison we're talking about?"

"Yes, it's called Diphenhydramine. It's a sleeping agent commonly used by people with insomnia. In regular doses used as directed, it's harmless. But taken in excessive amounts, and we have what you see here. However, it's quite possible that some sort of intensifier was used to speed the process," he said, gesturing to Turk's body.

Cassi glanced once more at Turk then straightened and shook hands with the doctor. "Thanks for everything, doc." She left the room, walked back to her car, and drove off. As she drove, Cassi began putting two and two together, contemplating the bizarre chain of events, which had engulfed her the past few days. The syndicate wasn't working anonymously. They wanted her to know it was their handiwork. And if they knew about her plan to put Turk in protective custody, then it was quite possible they might know about...

"Tina! Oh my God!" she cried, aloud. Putting the flashing light on her dashboard once again, Cassi stomped on the accelerator and streaked toward her home, praying she wasn't too late.

Tina had just finished making a pizza in the oven and was taking it out to let it cool when she heard a car pull up in the driveway. At first she thought it was Cassi, but something was wrong. When the car door slammed it sounded like more the one. Whoever was out there had tried to slam the doors in unison, but one had slammed a few seconds before the others. Tina was paralyzed by fear. She stood rooted to the floor and her heart rate quickened as she heard footsteps approaching the house. It wasn't until the doorbell rang that she snapped out of her trance.

Running into the bedroom, Tina hunted frantically for a weapon, any weapon to defend herself. The doorbell quit ringing and was replaced by heavy pounding and smashing against the door. Just when it seemed hopeless, she found a snub-nosed 38 revolver in one of the dresser drawers. Cracking the breech, she found that all six cylinders were full, and slapped the cylinder back into place just as the door splintered from its hinges and fell inward with a frightening crash.

Tina eased to the bedroom door and peered cautiously out. Four men were standing in the living room and one was heading for the bedroom. Gathering her courage, she stepped out from the room and fired her weapon, sending a bullet through the first invader's throat. The man fell to the floor with a grunt, as his sidekicks ducked for cover. Tina fired again, hitting another man in the arm as he reached for his gun. She ducked back into the room as she heard other guns cocking. "No!" shouted one of the men. "We take her alive."

Tina heard someone moving in the living room and cautiously glanced outside, only to have one of the men rush and tackle her, knocking her backward onto the bed. "No!" she screamed, as the attacker painfully twisted her wrist and wrenched the pistol out of her hand. He then put a forearm across her throat, choking her. "I got her." He said, looking over his shoulder.

"Hold her," said another man, moving toward her with a syringe needle. Panic-stricken, Tina struggled and struggled but the man's grip was too strong, and his weight pinned her to the bed. She closed her eyes tightly and waited for the needle to pierce her skin.

As the man neared Tina, someone wrapped an arm around his throat, grabbed his hand, and jerked it behind him so that the needle was now pointing toward his body. The attacker then forced the man to thrust the needle into his back, injecting himself with whatever he'd meant to put into Tina. He fell without a sound to the floor.

"Hurry up and stick her, will 'ya?" said the man holding Tina. "We ain't got all night!"

A pair of hands grabbed the man and roughly pulled him off her. Tina opened her eyes to see Cassi Day whip the man around and knee him in the groin. The man stooped over with a groan and Cassi gave him a hard karate chop to the base of his skull, knocking him cold. He fell with a thud. Coughing and gasping, Tina wearily propped herself onto her elbows, as her friend helped her into a sitting position. "Hurt bad?"

"No," answered Tina, rubbing her neck. He just choked me a bit."

Cassi hugged her friend. "Tina, I'm sorry...I'm so damn sorry."

"I'm okay, big sister. You see I didn't go down without a fight."

"Yeah," said Cassi looking around at the inert forms littering her home. She felt sicker now than when she'd visited Mickey that final time in the hospital. She'd already lost him, but to lose Tina, the little sister she never had, would've been too much to bear. "Listen, I gotta get you out of here," she said. "There are some friends of mine who live on the outskirts of town, who'll keep you safe until this thing blows over."

"No, I'm staying with you," protested Tina.

"You can't!" Cassi said, firmly. "Tina, it's gotten too dangerous and I won't take chances with your life."

"But I..."

"No buts. You're leaving and that's that." Just then one of the men Cassi had decked stirred and came to with a groan. Cassi looked down at him then grabbed him by his collar and jerked him to his feet. Through clenched teeth she snarled, "Come here, you!" She dragged the man into the living room, as Tina grabbed her fallen revolver and followed. Throwing the invader against a wall, Cassi put a forearm across his throat and drew back her fist. "Why was my friend targeted like this? Who sent you here? Talk!" she yelled, shaking him.

When the man didn't answer, Cassi's anger flared. Her knee shot up into his groin and she punched him hard across the jaw. "You're ticking me off, jerk!" She warned. I'm gonna ask you again and you'd better talk or I'm really gonna work you over. And I've got all night to do it."

"Okay, okay, just don't hit me again. I'll tell you." The man said. "We were just following orders to grab her, that's all."

Cassi tightened her grip on his throat. "Whose orders? Where were you taking her?"

"Freeman's. He wanted us to bring her to the complex." The trembling man said.

"What complex?" Cassi growled, her eyes narrowing.

"T-techno computer..." He stammered.

Cassi pulled out her Beretta and pointed it at the man. "Get over there!" she said, motioning with the weapon. The man moved over to where one of his sidekicks lay holding a bleeding gunshot wound in his arm and sat next to him on the floor. "Tina..."

"I'm way ahead of you, Cass," said Tina, her revolver already pointed at the attackers.

"Face down, hands away from your body!" Cassi barked. "Make it fast. My trigger finger's starting to itch."

The men did as she ordered and she switched pistols with Tina. Thumbing the safety off, she said, "Keep them covered. If they move, blow them away." Cassi went into the bedroom and dragged out the semiconscious form of the man who'd tried to drug Tina. She dumped him in a heap next to his accomplices then checked the man Tina shot first. He was dead. She then went to her car and called for a police wagon and an ambulance. When that was done, she took over from Tina and guarded the captives, while her exhausted friend tried to get some sleep.

Minutes later the police van pulled into the driveway, followed by an ambulance and another patrol car. When the officers and medics had completed their business, Cassi pulled a carton of milk from the refrigerator, filled a glass, and sat at her table. She'd drank half the glass when her friend, Officer Dan Stevenson, approached. "You look like you're about ready to pass out, Cassi. You need to get some rest."

"Believe me I want to", said Cassi, looking wearily at him. "But I've got..." She buried her face in her hands, too tired to finish her sentence. Dan put a hand on her shoulder.

"Listen, I'll post an unmarked car out here tonight and you and your friend can get some rest. How about it?" The thought of paperwork made her made her more tired than she was already. And she knew she'd be asleep at her desk before she finished half of it.

"Y'know something, that might not be such a bad idea. Thanks, Dan." Dan winked and went to his patrol car to make a radio call. An hour later, a red jeep drove up and parked near the edge of the driveway and Cassi and Dan went out to meet it. After Stevenson informed the two plain-clothed officers of the situation, he and Cassi thanked them. Giving Dan a light pat on the shoulder, the weary detective went back into her home and propped her door back up as best she could. She then turned off the lights and fell drowsily onto the couch, placing her pistol within easy reach, should she need it. She was asleep as soon as her head hit the pillow.

Days later, Cassi was called into Warden's office. When she entered, she found her captain seated amongst two men she didn't know. One black, the other white, but both were wearing suits. "You wanted to see me, captain?"

"Yes, detective," said Warden. These are agents Thompson and Wilkes, FBI." The two men nodded to Cassi and she returned the gesture, as Warden handed her a sheet of paper. "You'd better have a look at this," he said. Cassi scanned the document briefly then abruptly looked at Warden, astonished.

"Federal indictment?"

"Yes, detective," said Wilkes, folding his arms. "I don't think you're fully aware of what you're dealing with here."

Cassi placed the document on Warden's desk and turned to Wilkes, her hands on her hips. "I'm aware that I'm dealing with a murdering syndicate that's killed my partner and pumps poison through the streets. Is there something you feds know that I don't?"

"As a matter of fact, there are several things," said Thompson, his hands clasped in front of him. "But we want to hear what you know first."

"I just told you," said Cassi, looking at him. "How about enlightening me some more, gentlemen?"

Thompson looked at Wilkes, who nodded slightly. "Does the name Scorpio mean anything to you, lieutenant?"

"Yeah, he heads this syndicate that murdered my partner." Cassi said.

"Well, this syndicate, the Omega Syndicate as it's called, has its hands in just about every kind of dirt you can think of, lieutenant," said Thompson. "Drugs, racketeering, prostitution, slavery, you name it."

"Well this is all very informative, gentlemen," quipped Cassi. "But would you mind telling me what this indictment has to do with me?"

"They also deal in terrorism, detective," said Wilkes. "They supply every terrorist organization in the world with our guns. They also import foreign weapons and sell them at extortionist prices on the black market."

Cassi was getting impatient. "You still haven't told me what this has to do with me."

"We've read your reports concerning this case, lieutenant. You've harbored a key informant, Thomas Kirk, alias Turk, who might have led us to some other information we could have used, caused the deaths of several good officers, and put an innocent girl, one Christina Colton, in danger as well," said Thompson.

"Lieutenant, I can't stand by you on this one." Warden said, sadly. "You're off the case."

"What?" Cassi said, incredulously. "Captain, you can't be serious. I've been through too much and other officers have died, helping us out. You can't take me off this case, not when I'm this close." But when she looked into Warden's eyes, she knew her efforts were futile.

Warden continued. "You'll take a mandatory vacation without pay until this matter can be resolved."

"You want my shield, captain?"

" Not yet," said Warden.

Cassi glanced at the federal agents once more then went to the door. She opened it halfway and then turned to face the agents. "By the way, how long have you been after Scorpio?"

"Four years now, why?" said Thompson.

"Yeah, well if you haven't caught him in all that time, you must be doing something seriously wrong, agent man." And with that, Cassi closed the door behind her and walked out of the building to her car.

CHAPTER 12

FIRST STRIKE

The two men faced each other from opposite sides of the huge room, their muscles tensing as they slowly advanced forward. Sweat rolled down the faces and bodies of both men and their eyes narrowed in anticipation of each other's move. Suddenly one man lunged forward with a back fist strike, followed by a round kick a spinning back kick.

Scorpio dodged and blocked the man's attacks with ease then did a round kick, which caught the man in the side of his head, spinning him around. Scorpio then jabbed with his left hand and did a spinning back fist strike, which struck the unprepared man across the cheek. Still reeling from the blow, the man was caught off guard by a jumping sidekick from Scorpio, which sent him staggering backward.

Unable to regain his balance, the man fell against the wall, banging his head as he did. He sank unconsciously to the floor. "This concludes our lesson for today." Scorpio said. Scorpio made a beckoning gesture with one hand and two men, who'd been watching from outside, came in and carried the man's inert form from the room. No sooner than they'd left, when Freeman walked into the room.

"Yes, Mr. Freeman?" inquired Scorpio, standing ramrod straight.

"I don't think miss Day will be a problem for us anymore," said Freeman.

"Indeed, how so?"

"I've been informed that she's been suspended from duty and taken off this particular case. Those two idiots, Thompson and Wilkes are handling the case now."

"We'll elude them as always," said Scorpio, striding over to the small refrigerator in one corner of the room. He pulled a bottle of tea out of the refrigerator, opened it and took a long pull. When he finished drinking, he wiped sweat from his face. "Is there anything else, Mr. Freeman?"

The answer was a long time coming. "No, sir." He turned to go.

"And one more thing, Mr. Freeman," Scorpio said. "Even though detective Day has been suspended, there's too much at risk to allow her to interfere. "Send her another message." A dangerous smile crossed Freeman's face.

"Yes, sir." he said. He exited the room, leaving Scorpio to finish toweling off.

Cassi couldn't believe what had happened to her, as she drove along. She'd come closer in two months to cracking this particular case than the FBI had in four years, only to be pulled off it and suspended. She'd never been a glory seeker, but then again she'd never been one to sit on the sidelines and let others make the touchdowns either. The situation was extremely frustrating.

So preoccupied with her own troubled thoughts, Cassi just barely hit her brakes in time to keep from hitting the car in front of her, which had stopped at a red light. *Get a grip, Cass,* she thought to herself. *Take it easy now.* The light changed and she drove on. She pulled into a filling station to get some gas and while she was refueling, her mind drifted back to the incident a few nights ago. If the Omega Syndicate was as powerful as the FBI said, why didn't they send enough people to kill her and Tina if they thought the two ladies were that big a threat? Were they sending her a message, or just toying with her? Cassi didn't know, but one thing she was certain of, nobody was going to kill her partner, kick in her door and hurt her friends, without getting some payback, whether she was on the case or not.

Cassi finished refueling, paid the clerk, and was on her way again. She'd gone only a few miles when she noticed a black jeep with tinted windows following her in the dusk. It hadn't caught up with her yet, but it was moving steadily between the lanes, coming closer and closer. Cassi pulled her pistol from its holster and laid it on the seat next to her as the dark vehicle neared.

Suddenly the jeep sped up and pulled next to her. The passenger window rolled down and a gun muzzle poked out. Cassi quickly braked and let the jeep rush past her but not before the weapon discharged and the bullet whacked into the doorpost of her car. "Oh brother," she groaned. "My mechanic's gonna love this."

The jeep cut in front of her and she stomped the accelerator, bumping the jeep hard from the rear. The enemy vehicle served back and forth, veering into the next lane then back in front of Cassi's car. Tires screeched and horns from other vehicles blared in protest as Cassi accelerated, switched lanes and cut in front of her attackers. She saw a small two-lane street off to her right and steered onto it, leading the jeep away from the innocents. She looked into her rearview window at the pursuing vehicle. "That's right," She hissed between clenched teeth. "Keep following me!"

The jeep sped up and gunfire erupted from the passenger side, but Cassi moved back and forth between the lanes, dodging the assault. The enemy vehicle then changed tactics by racing up alongside Cassi's car ramming her from side trying to run her off the road. Rather than wrestle with the other vehicle, Cassi did the next best thing and accelerated ahead, she hit the brakes and turned sharply, going into an 180 degree spin. Now her vehicle was facing the enemy's. Cassi stomped the accelerator and sent her trans AM charging forward. Grabbing her pistol from the seat, she aimed out the window and fired at the oncoming vehicle.

Two bullets pierced the windshield on the driver's side of the jeep as Cassi's car roared past. Tires squealed and the night air was filled with the acrid smells of burned rubber and cordite as Cassi hit the brakes and spun around again, ready to give her attackers another run. But now the jeep was swerving back and forth across the street, out of control. The terrified passenger tried to steady the speeding vehicle, but to no avail, the jeep turned too sharply, flipped over several times and landed on its side in a ditch. Cassi got out of her car and ran toward the wrecked vehicle in hopes of rescuing someone for questioning, gun ready just in case one of them was still able to take a pot shot at her. But when she saw the flame burning on the underside of the jeep, she knew she'd never make it in time.

She'd barely taken cover when the dark vehicle exploded in flames, throwing her to the ground. Cassi lay still as fiery debris from the jeep rained down around her. Then, with her ears ringing, she climbed slowly to her feet, gazing at the smoldering, twisted wreckage in front of her. She turned and jogged toward her car. With the driver's door still open, Cassi sat behind the wheel and keyed he radio. She was about to call in the incident when a startling realization hit her.

During the chaos she'd forgotten that she'd been suspended. And though many of the officers knew her, several more didn't. Depending upon which officers responded to the call, she didn't know if they'd view the matter as self-defense once they arrived. She'd already been federally indicted earlier that day, and this action was sure to land her behind bars if the feds caught up with her. And what was worse, if she left the scene, she'd look guilty.

Cassi was still contemplating her situation when she felt a gun muzzle touch the back of her head. As the trigger cocked she glanced up into the rearview mirror and saw a man in a dark outfit glaring at her from the back seat. Cassi looked at the blood on the side of his face and concluded that he was one of the attackers from the jeep. He must have jumped clear before the explosion.

"Do what I say, or spend the rest of your life dead," he snarled. Given her situation, Cassi decided to play along.

"Okay, Okay. J-just don't hurt me, alright?" she said, pretending to be scared.

"Close the door," said the man. "You and me are gonna take little ride."

Cassi did as the man said and started the car. Putting the car in gear, she drove down the street, at a slow, steady pace.

"Hey, speed it up!" the man said, annoyed. "I don't want any cops sneaking up on us."

"You're the boss," said Cassi, and she floored the accelerator. The sudden burst of speed caught the man off guard and he fell backward, his pistol going awry. Cassi grabbed her pistol from the seat and hit the brakes, causing the man to bump his already throbbing head. Suddenly he found himself staring into the muzzle of Cassi's Beretta. "Neat trick," quipped Cassi. "But mine was better."

"So what are you gonna do, shoot me?" said the man.

"If you don't drop that pistol, that's exactly what I'm gonna do!" warned Cassi. "You and your cronies have already tried to kill me tonight, so don't test me!"

Realizing that he had no chance, the man let his gun fall to the floor and raised his hands, surrendering. Keeping her pistol on him, Cassi opened the door and backed out of the car. "Come out of there!"

Wincing in pain, the man crawled over the seat and toward the open driver's door. When he was halfway out of the door, Cassi grabbed him by the collar, jerked him off the seat, and threw him up against the car. With her pistol pressed against the back of his head, she frisked him for more weapons then handcuffed him. She positioned the man on his stomach outside the car and called in to the station. Minutes later, the police and fire units arrived.

The officers jumped out of their car and walked slowly toward Cassi, pointing their weapons. "Hands above your head, Miss," said one of them. Cassi glanced at them and sure enough they were officers she didn't know..."It's alright I'm a cop." She said, wearily.

The first officer cocked his pistol. "Miss, I'm not gonna tell you again. Put your hands above your head!"

I'm too tired to put my hands above my head!" She snapped. "Now if you're not too blind to see, my gun and badge are on top of my car!" Keeping Cassi covered, the first officer motioned with his head. "Check it out, Mel." Mel holstered his weapon and walked over to check her credentials. After a quick inspection, he looked back at his partner and nodded.

The lead officer holstered his pistol and came around the car to where Cassi's attacker lay cuffed. "Whoa," he said, looking down at the immobilized figure. "Just what's going on here?"

Cassi reached down and hauled the prisoner to his feet. "Better break out the pads and pencils, boys. It's a long story."

CHAPTER 13

ASSAULT

Cassi Day closed and locked her newly repaired and reinforced door upon arriving home. The incidents of the previous hours, from the chase to dealing with the police after the gunfight, left her so drained and fatigued that she could barely stand. On her way to the kitchen, she removed her jacket and laid it on the couch. Cassi had finished eating and was drinking some milk when the phone rang. Setting her glass down, she answered it. "Yeah?"

"Greetings, miss Day," said a frigid voice.

"Who is this?"

"Oh come now, detective. You've met several of my associates already."

Cassi sat up straight and her eyes narrowed "Scorpio!" She whispered, angrily.

"Very perceptive. I'll get right to the point, Miss Day. That little show tonight was just to get your attention. By now you must know that my network is vast. However, I do admire your resourcefulness and resilience and that's why I'm offering you a position in my organization."

"Organization?" said Cassi. "Syndicate, you mean."

"If you will," allowed Scorpio. "You'll make more money in an hour than you would in a year as a police officer, should you choose to work for me. If not, you saw what happened to your partner and the one called Turk. I'm offering you the keys to an empire, Miss Day."

Cassi rolled her eyes, disgusted. "Do me a favor, Scorpio, shove it!" And she slammed the phone down with a bang.

Later before going to bed, Cassi practiced a few martial arts katas, (forms of exercise), to calm herself. She concentrated mainly on her breathing, which was essential to executing correct moves. Breathing in through her nose and exhaling out through her lips, she executed a three-punch attack, following a low high kick, and finished with a jumping spinning crescent kick. Having dealt with the imaginary opponents in front of her, Cassi then executed a back kick to ward off a rear assault and jumping split kick to stop a simultaneous rush from both sides.

Her katas finished, the young lady knelt Japanese style on the floor and closed her eyes in meditation, taking slow, deep breaths. Her muscles relaxed and tension slowly left her body as she continued her breathing, clearing her mind. Minutes later Cassi turned out the bedroom light and prepared her bed. She'd said her prayers and was about to get into bed when something eclipsed the moonlight shining into her bedroom.

Slowly easing her pistol from the nightstand, Cassi crept cautiously to her window and peered out into the darkness. At first she saw nothing in the pale moonlight then a shadow to her left moved and she saw a man aiming a weapon at her. She ducked just barely in time before he fired and two bullets tore through her window. One buried itself into the corner of her doorpost and the other whacked into the fireplace. Having dropped into a prone position, Cassi leaped to her feet, raced to the front door, and hurriedly unlocked it. Weapon ready, she flung the door open and ran out into the yard.

Gunfire blossomed from a van parked behind her car. And Cassi ducked around the corner as bullets glanced off the concrete of her house. Leaning around the corner, she fired back, blowing out the passenger's window. The gunman who'd been on foot came around the house and got behind her in hopes of flushing her toward the van, but Cassi executed a back kick, hitting him in the stomach. Spinning quickly around, she kicked the weapon out of his hand and covered him with her own. Hearing footsteps coming toward her, Cassi wrapped an arm around the gunman's throat, got behind him, and placed her weapon against his head as the attackers came around the corner, brandishing their weapons. For a moment it was a stand off but then the men chambered rounds in their guns. And she knew they'd shoot her and her makeshift hostage.

The next few minutes seemed to pass in slow motion as Cassi Day fought for her life in the darkness. Using her hostage as a human shield, she fired her pistol and dropped both men before they could fire a shot. Then, putting the man in a full nelson, she advanced toward the van, still shielded by his body. More gunfire erupted from the van and the attacker's body was riddled with bullets as Cassi continued her advance.

She shot from behind the dead man, one bullet hitting and killing the van driver and she heard the engine block crack as another bullet smashed through the vehicles fender. Having advanced far enough, Cassi flung the bloody, lifeless form to the ground and took cover behind her car.

"You, in the van!" she yelled. "Come out slowly with your hands where I can see them, now!" Silence was her only answer. Cassi came around her car and toward the now silent van, weapon at the ready. She flung the enemy vehicle's doors open and found only dead bodies within. Sirens blared as two police cruisers rushed in and stopped at the end of her driveway. Four uniformed officers jumped out and ran toward the house as Cassi, blood spattered and trembling, sank wearily to her knees on the grass.

"Hold it right there, miss!" said one of the officers, pointing his weapon at her

"Scott, it's okay. I know her. She's a cop," said a female voice.

The young lady then knelt down and gently shook Cassi's shoulders. "Cassi, it's Vanessa. Are you Okay?"

Cassi blinked away her blurring vision and looked at her friend. "Va-Vanessa?"

Vanessa Roberts smiled slightly. "Yeah, it's me. Are you hurt?"

Cassi wearily shook her head. Then, overcome with fatigue, her eyes rolled back into their sockets and she fell into Vanessa's arms.

"Oh God!" said Vanessa, stricken with fear." Scott, help me with her."

When Cassi awoke she was in a hospital. She blinked a few times and her blurred vision slowly began to clear, but when she tried to sit up a strong hand restrained her.

"You need to rest, lieutenant. You've had some kind of night," said a male voice. Cassi couldn't make out the person's face due to her still blurred vision, and his voice sounded like a 45 record on speed 33.

"Who are you?" she asked, warily.

"A friend," came the answer. "Now get some rest, lieutenant. You need it." Cassi closed her eyes once more and then opened them very slowly and her vision cleared completely and she saw Matthew Warden looking down at her. She relaxed and smiled faintly. "How long have I been here?"

"About ten hours," said Warden. "The doctor said you have a moderate case of fatigue, not too serious. You can go home in a day or so."

"How'd I get here?"

"Officer Vanessa Roberts and her partner brought you," answered Warden. Cassi nodded and glanced out the window at the gray clouds and rain drenched streets as Warden pulled up a chair and sat next to her bed.

"Lieutenant, if you feel up to talking, what exactly happened last night?"

"It all started with that call I got from Scorpio..."

"Wait a second," interrupted Warden. "He called you?"

"Yeah, he offered me a position in the syndicate, and of course I turned it down. Then later I was getting ready to hit the sack, and these goons jumped me, the rest you know."

Warden sat back in his chair and thought for a moment then looked back at Cassi. "You know what this means, don't you?"

"Yeah, he's got a contract out on me." Answered Cassi.

"Precisely," said Warden. "Which means I'm going to have to put you in protective custody."

Cassi held up her hand. "Whoa cap, I appreciate your efforts, but I'm a big girl and can take care of myself. Besides, you can't spare the manpower. Just about every officer you got is wrapped up in this case as it is. I'll have to watch my own back."

Warden knew she was right. He stood up, put his chair back where he'd gotten it, then turned to her, speaking low in case anyone was listening outside the door. "Alright, if that's how you want it. But I am posting a guard here tonight, just in case. After that, you watch yourself, hear me?"

Cassi nodded and winked. "Thanks, cap." Warden waved and left the room, closing the door behind him. Glancing at her watch, which read 6:45, Cassi lay back, closed her eyes and slept.

Security officer, Brian Diggs, dozed in his chair as he sat outside Cassi's door later that night. Struggling to keep awake, he got up, stretched, and walked to the vending machine around the corner for some coffee. He removed his cap and scratched his brown hair as his blue eyes scanned the machine. He made his selection and while the cups filled, called to the duty nurse.

"Hey, Alexis, want some coffee?"

"No, thanks," she called back. "How about a shot of Jack Daniels?"

"Yeah, right." Diggs said, chuckling at her joke. He was just about to go back to his post when he felt something stab him in the neck. His cup dropped to the floor and the hot liquid splashed in all directions as he clutched his neck and turned to see a man dressed as a doctor holding a needle. Diggs reached for a weapon on his utility belt, but his reflexes were sluggish and he was losing consciousness. As he began to fall, another man rushed from the stairwell and caught the drugged guard before he hit he floor.

"Get rid of him," said the doctor. "I'll finish up here." The other man nodded and dragged the unconscious officer into the stairwell. While the "Doctor" filled a new syringe from a vile in his lab coat and started for Cassi's room.

"Making a late round, doctor?" said Alexis as he passed by her desk.

"Oh yes, I thought I'd look in on Miss Day and see how she's coming along." He said, with a mock look of concern. Just then the nurse's intercom beeped and she answered,

"Yes?"

"I...I need something for pain," said a shaky voice on the other end. The nurse checked the panel on the desk and room 912 was flashing.

"Excuse me, doctor," she said, standing. She went to the medicine tray next to the desk, took a couple of pills from one of the tray's pockets, and disappeared down the hallway.

As Alexis entered the dark room she received a sharp blow to the back of her head, and fell to the floor in a heap. The attacker then pulled her inert body out of sight and waved to the "doctor" who nodded and slowly entered Cassi's room. Removing the needle from his coat, the man edged closed and closer to her sleeping form, eagerly anticipating the moment he would inject his poison into her. He pulled back the covers and found, to his surprise, only pillows.

Cassi suddenly lunged from the shadows and delivered a karate chop to the base of his skull, knocking him onto the bed. Though caught off guard, the man didn't drop the needle. Still lying halfway on the bed, he rolled over and, using both feet, kicked young woman away from him. Cassi staggered backward and fell against the door with a thud, as her attacker leaped off the bed and rushed her, his hand drawn back for an overhand stab.

Crossing her arms high in front of her, she parried the attack and kicked the man in the groin. Acting quickly, Cassi grabbed the man's knife hand with her left hand, drew back, and smashed him hard in the face with her right elbow. Blood spurted from his broken nose, as he twisted and fell onto the bed once more. The man felt a sharp, stinging pain in his stomach and pushing himself off the bed, looked down to see the handle of his own syringe protruding from his body. He jerked the needle free and turned slowly around to face Cassi, who was poised in a defensive martial arts stance. The man blinked twice, fell to his knees, and then collapsed onto his side. The last thing he saw before he died was the empty syringe lying next to him, on the floor.

Cassi sighed deeply, still looking at the dead body lying before her. But she knew she couldn't rest. Where there was one killer, there may be others. She cautiously opened the door and peered out. A balding man in a gray jacket, blue slacks, and dark shoes was coming down the hallway toward her, twisting a silencer into the muzzle of his pistol.

Cassi knew she had to act quickly. Ducking out the door, she charged across the hallway, veered left, and smashed the stairwell door open with her shoulder. She took off down the stairs just a bullet whizzed behind her head and blew out the small window inside the door. When she'd outrun him a bit, she hid behind a flight of stairs and waited, her heart pounding. Sure enough, the man came down the stairs in pursuit, looking around wildly for her.

Cassi waited until the man came down her stairs then jumped out and kicked the weapon out of the startled man's hand. Before he could react, she karate chopped him across the throat and swung a hard left to the temple, dropping him like a ton of bricks. "Don't hunt what you can't kill." She quipped to the unconscious man. She heard a scream come from upstairs and knew someone had found the body in her room. Stepping over the fallen man, she eased into the hallway, looking cautiously around. She saw a women's restroom off to her right and darted into it.

She was momentarily safe but she knew she couldn't stay there forever. She had to get out of the hospital and fast...but how?" She backed slowly away from the door and fabric of some sort brushed against her as she neared the wall. Cassi turned around and saw several nurse uniforms hanging from a rack. Stripping off the blood stained hospital gown, she hurriedly put on one of the uniforms. She looked around for a pair of shoes but could find none, so she went around the corner to the locker room, hoping against hope that her luck would improve. She searched every unlocked locker she found and just when she was about to give up, she found a pair of white pumps. The shoes were a bit big on her, but after she stuffed some tissue into the toes they were a perfect fit.

Alarms squawked and a nurse chattered over the loud speakers telling patients to remain in their rooms. "I repeat, there is a code red of floor nine. All patients are advised to stay in their rooms until further notice."

Cassi just finished putting her hair into a makeshift ponytail when a doctor burst into the room. "Hey," she said, urgently. "Didn't you hear? They've got a real mess upstairs and they need everyone available. That means you, nurse!"

Cassi slapped on a nurse's cap and trotted to the door, held ajar by the doctor. As she passed by, the doctor said," And nurse, lower the hem in that skirt. That is not hospital standard."

Cassi stopped and looked down at herself briefly. The short, snug-fitting garment made her look more like a hooker than a nurse, but she decided not to bicker. She looked back at the doctor and said, "Yes, doctor." as meekly as her temper would allow. She then stepped into the stairwell and was gone.

With chaos erupting all around her Cassi Day activated one of the fire alarms and made her way down the stairs to the first floor. *That ought to keep them busy for a while*, she thought. She was about to open the door when three police officers entered the double doors from the street. Cassi stepped back and flattened herself against the wall beside the door so they wouldn't see her as they jogged past. Peeking through the window to make sure they'd all past, she slipped into the hallway and out the double doors.

A light rain was falling outside, accompanied by a chilly breeze as Cassi stood on the curb outside the building. She knew this hospital well and it was a good two miles from her home. And though she could easily have walked the distance, she didn't want to do so in this miserable weather. She walked around the corner and down the sidewalk, hoping to find someone she knew from the police force to hitch a ride with. Amid the indistinctive chatter and flashing red and blue lights of police and medical vehicles, Cassi walked through the crowd of police, security officers and medics virtually unnoticed, but for a few lustful glances from some of the men, who were looking at her legs. Finding no one to help her, she continued on until she came to the emergency entrance.

Passing an ambulance, she looked toward the parking lot and saw a sight that nearly threw her into spasms. There, parked next to a black, Chevy truck, was her Trans AM. She shook her head and chuckled slightly. "Thanks, Vanessa," she whispered.

Walking briskly through the drizzle, Cassi went to the rear of the car, knelt down, and pulled a small magnetic box from the underside of the vehicle and removed the spare key from within. She got into the car and was about to turn the ignition when a frightening thought occurred.

Since the day she'd found the note on Turk's body, she'd taken every possible precaution, one of which included placing a piece of transparent tape on the hood of her car as a "Just in case." Cassi grabbed a flashlight from the glove compartment, got out, and went to the hood to check it. Running her fingers along the crack where the hood would open, she found that the tape seal had definitely been broken. She opened the hood and turned on her flashlight. Attached to her engine was a bomb, set to detonate the very moment she turned the ignition. *Why am I not surprised?* she thought to herself.

She inwardly thanked God for the time she'd spent on the bomb squad, learning about specific explosives and detonation devices. This one happened to be one she was familiar with and she was able to disarm it easily. With rain soaking through her clothes, Cassi pulled the wires in sequence and lifted the deadly device from the engine. Checking the car to make sure no more were attached, the young detective got into her car, started the engine and headed home, leaving the chattering mob behind her.

CHAPTER 14

A HAND UP

The next morning as Cassi was taking a can of TAB soda from the refrigerator, she saw someone walking outside her living room window. Whoever it was, was walking across the front lawn, occasionally pausing and looking at the house, as if trying to see if anyone was inside. Setting her drink down, she yanked her Beretta from her belt and crept outside. Striding quietly up to the ebony-skinned man, Cassi pointed her weapon at him and cocked the trigger. The man turned slowly around and she found herself staring into the face of FBI agent Michael Wilkes.

"Pretty jumpy for a cop," he said.

Cassi unlocked her weapon and put it back into her belt. "And you're pretty stealthy for a suit."

"Oh, I try to keep in practice. Looks like you made some enemies, lieutenant," he said, looking at where the bullets had knocked some of the concrete from her house.

"Comes with the job," said Cassi, as they walked to the carport. "But I'm not telling you anything you don't already know, am I?"

"No." said Wilkes, putting his hands in his pockets.

"So what's your game, Wilkes? You didn't come out here just to pay me a social call."

"I came to offer my assistance," Wilkes said. "You see, I'm not the Uncle Tom type when it comes to following regulations."

Cassi leaned against her car and folded her arms. "Get to the point."

"After reading your file and talking with your captain, you're the perfect person to help with this case."

"I see," Cassi snorted. "So that's why you indicted me and pulled me off it, huh?"

"Perhaps we were a bit hasty in doing so, but we had to find out how much you knew and how close you were getting."

"Go on." Cassi said.

"As I'm sure you're well aware, Scorpio has a very powerful network. But I've got some connections and equipment that'll give us an edge. Since he's familiar with our top agents, we'll need someone we can infiltrate into his ranks to find out something we can use against him. That's where your undercover expertise comes in."

Cassi stood, her hands on her hips. "Suppose I say no."

Wilkes glanced down, scratched his ear, and then looked back at Cassi. "Then you're a dead woman, Miss Day. And Scorpio's already got a coffin picked out."

Cassi opened her car door and pulled out the disarmed bomb that the syndicate men had put under her hood and tossed it to Wilkes. "As you can see, he's already tried to ice me and I'm still standing."

"I wouldn't break my arm patting myself on the back if I were you, lieutenant." Warned Wilkes. "Scorpio's just playing with you right now, but sooner or later he's going to get tired and when that happens, you'll be finished before you know it. I know what I'm talking about because he's killed some of our best agents, four of which were friends of mine...just like your friend, officer Colton."

"I'm not one of your agents!" Cassi said. She walked a few steps away from him, contemplating what Wilkes had said, then turned and looked back at him. "Okay, I'm in, but not because I need you, or because I'm afraid of Scorpio. I want to nail the creep as badly as you do."

"Well then, how about we discuss this someplace more private?"

"Alright," said Cassi. And together they went into the house.

Hours later, after they'd made a tentative plan, Cassi and Wilkes drove to the police station for a private talk with captain Warden. Once in his office, they locked the door, closed the blinds, and sat down to discuss their plans with him.

"Since lieutenant Day is on suspension, or rather mandatory vacation, she'll be able to travel abroad and get us the information we need to bring them down once and for all." Wilkes said.

Warden leaned forward and resting his forearms on his desk, glanced at Cassi, then at Wilkes. "And just where are you planning to send her?"

"You remember that business card you gave me a few days ago?" said Cassi.

"The Techno Computer Facility? Sure, what about it?" asked Warden.

"That's where I want to start looking. Maybe I can kick over a few rocks out there."

"And my guess is that you want to go to the main branch in Los Angeles."

"You got it," confirmed Cassi. "The way I look at it, Scorpio's got half the underworld population in Santa Bella looking for me, so I'll go where he least expects...right to his front door."

"I don't like this." Warden said to Wilkes "Too many things could go wrong out there, even if she is being monitored by the FBI."

Cassi uncrossed her legs and sat up straighter. "Since when are you the nervous type, cap? Besides when I signed up for undercover, I didn't expect a picnic."

"Captain, I know she's your best officer, but let's be logical." Wilkes intervened. "We're talking about a man of tremendous intellect and charisma, who's capable of wiping out thousands of people with a snap of his fingers and somehow manage an air-tight alibi, making him mister untouchable. If we don't take this opportunity and nail him now, we may not get another. He'll murder more people, blow up evidence of his crimes and disappear in the flames. Detective Day is our best, and probably our only chance at this."

Warden drummed his fingertips on his desk, thinking about what Wilkes had said and the situation they were facing. And though he didn't want to admit it, he knew Wilkes was right. "All right. What's your plan?"

"Simple, we'll outfit Miss Day and infiltrate her into his organization. From there, she'll dig through some personal files and hopefully find something we can use against Scorpio."

Warden looked at Wilkes incredulously as he slowly rose from his chair. "Hopefully? And what if she doesn't find anything? If her cover's blown, she's history!"

"That's a chance I'm gonna have to take," said Cassi. "It's no different from what I do here."

"You're sure this is what you want to do?" asked Warden. "LA's a whole new ball park."

Cassi stood and locked eyes with Warden. "I'm positive I want to do this. Captain, I've got to...for Mickey."

"Wilkes, let us have this room," said Warden. "Grab yourself some coffee or something." The FBI agent nodded and left the office, closing the door behind him as, Warden turned to Cassi. "Lieutenant, your partner didn't ask you to fight his battles for him when he was alive, and I'm sure he's not asking for that now. How are you going to honor him if you get yourself killed out there?"

"You're just gonna have to trust me on this, cap." said Cassi. "I've never let you down before, have I?" Warden was silent. Although he didn't show it, he was being torn apart inside, First Mickey was murdered, and now Cassi was running off to battle the very syndicate that had killed him, knowing full well that she'd wind up dead too if she ever slipped up. He'd never told Cassi how he'd felt, but if he'd had a daughter, he'd want it to be her. He just couldn't bring himself to say so. After a long moment of silence, Warden walked over and gently gripped her shoulders.

"You come back here alive, you hear me?"

Cassi gave him that wicked, reckless grin that she was famous for throughout the department. "Me, get killed and miss a chance to rattle your cage some more, no way." She said, winking.

Days later, wearing a black blouse with matching slacks and black pumps, Cassi stood outside the department with two packed bags next to her. Restless, she paced slowly back and forth on the sidewalk checking her watch as she waited for Wilkes to arrive. Within minutes a brown Buick pulled up in front of her and Wilkes stepped out.

"Ready to ride?" he said.

"Yeah," said Cassi, picking up her bags. Wilkes unlocked the trunk and taking the bags from her, placed them inside as Cassi walked around to the cab and got in. Wilkes closed the trunk and joined her in the cab. From his office window Warden watched as the car drove into traffic and was soon lost from view, mentally praying for his beautiful, headstrong officer.

CHAPTER 15

INFILTRATION

Scorpio sat at a table with four of his lieutenants, including Nick Freeman. The mood was grim and serious, which was normal for any of Scorpio's meetings, but a sense of intensity hung in the air around the seated men like a thick fog. Sitting ram-rod straight. Scorpio placed his forearms on the polished table, his cold blue eyes moving back and forth among the assembled men before he spoke.

"Gentlemen, we have a problem, and her name is Cassi Day," he said, interlacing his fingers. "For those of you who don't already know, she's an elite operative with the Santa Bella police department, who's already killed or incarcerated most of our associates. She's also responsible for the debacle in Burbank as well as the catastrophe at the warehouse. She's resourceful, intelligent, and relentless, which make her dangerous quarry."

Upon hearing this statement, some of the men shifted in their chairs, glancing nervously at one another, except for Freeman who, having already tangled with her, kept his attention on his boss. "However," continued Scorpio, "I want her here, and I want her alive. I don't care what it takes nor do I want any excuses. Is that understood?" The men nodded nervously. "Good, then execute." One by one the men rose, replaced their chairs, and left the room.

The long ride from Santa Bella had caught up with Cassi as she sat next to Wilkes. She yawned and stretched then looked out the window at the scenery as the car drove through the Los Angeles streets.

"How long before we go to work?" she asked, wearily.

"Not for a couple of days yet?" said Wilkes. "I've called ahead and everything's been arranged, but I figured you might want to rest up a bit."

" I'll be all right," said Cassi, stifling another yawn.

"Sure you will, look at you. You can barely keep your eyes open," said Wilkes.

"If I were you detective, I'd get as much rest as possible because once we start this, there'll be little time for it. But I'm not telling you anything you don't already know, am I?" Cassi looked over at Wilkes, who grinned as he turned a corner and chuckled at his statement, returning her gaze to the streets.

They kept driving until they came to a motel in one of the seedier areas of the city. Most of the buildings were painted with colored graffiti, some of which were talented, comic book-style works while others were gang symbols and or vulgar communication. Wilkes parked the car and cut the engine. "The other agents will meet us here," he said.

"How many more are coming?" asked Cassi.

"Four," said Wilkes, looking at her. "In fact, some of them should already have checked in. Let's go check it out." Cassi opened the door but before she got out, Wilkes touched her shoulder. "Watch yourself in this area." Cassi nodded and together they stepped out into the late evening sunlight and headed toward the motel.

While they were en route, several Black and Latino men were eyeing Cassi and some were even whistling at her. Some of the Latinos were nudging their friends with their elbows and chattering in their native language, smiling at her. Cassi inwardly bristled at the treatment, but controlled her anger for sake of the mission.

They entered the motel and Wilkes rang the bell for the clerk as Cassi leaned against the counter next to him, occasionally glancing outside at the population. Wilkes rang the bell again and an obese, bald man came waddling over to the desk from the back office. "Take a chill pill, man. I'm coming," he said, annoyed. "Whatta ya need?"

"Yes, I've got some friends coming in from out of town and we're supposed to meet here. I was wondering if they'd checked in yet," said Wilkes

"Names?" said the clerk, opening his reservation book. "Sheila Jenkins, Bill Coleman, Rick Masters, and Lee Anderson," answered Wilkes.

The clerk scanned the book for a few moments then looked up and said, "Yeah, they're all in house."

Wilkes nodded and said, "That'll work. My wife here and I'd like to check in." The clerk placed a registration card on the desk and Wilkes filled it out, signing the names John and Kimberly Thomas, Wilkes then paid the security deposit and the nightly rate and he and Cassi went back to the car, got their luggage and went to their room. Once inside, Wilkes pulled a small radio from his coat pocket and extended the wire while Cassi set her luggage in a corner and looked out the window.

"This is Wilkes. We're here."

"Roger," said a voice on the other end." We copy." Wilkes pushed the wire back down and pocketed his radio. "The rest of the team will be here shortly, detective," he said. Cassi looked back at him and nodded then closed the blinds and sat at the small table near the window. She removed her sunglasses, yawned and gently rubbed her tired eyes.

There was a knock at the door and Wilkes went to answer it as Cassi stood. He looked through the peek hole then unlocked the door and a tall, blue-eyed brunette stepped into the room, followed by three other men. Wilkes turned to Cassi and gestured to his team. "This is Tawny Campbell, alias Sheila Jenkins, William Roberts, alias Bill Coleman, Randle Chase, alias Rick Masters, and Steven Weathers, alias Lee Anderson." Cassi shook hands with the team as Wilkes continued, "Everybody, this is detective Cassi Day, Santa Bella PD. She's the operative helping us."

"Your reputation precedes you," said Tawny. "If you're even one-eighth as good as your files indicate, it's going to be an honor working with you, lieutenant. "

"Thanks." Cassi said, as the other agents nodded their approval.

"Well, I don't know about the rest of you," said Tawny. "But after all that traveling, I've got the munchies like you wouldn't believe. What say we grab something to eat and then go over the plans?"

"Sounds good to me," said Weathers, rubbing his growling stomach. He grinned sheepishly as his stomach continued growling.

Roberts chuckled at Weathers and Scratched the stubble of colorless beard on his face and said, "Weathers, where do you put all that food? You eat like horse and you're still rail-thin."

"Guess I just got a high metabolism," said Weathers.

Impatiently, Wilkes interrupted. "Okay then it's settled. We'll go grab something and then get the ball rolling. "You brought everything?"

"Roger that," said Randle chase, nodding.

"Then let's get going," said Wilkes, opening the door. One by one the federal operatives excited the room, talking in low tones amongst themselves. Cassi was the last to leave. Wilkes closed the door behind her and together they followed the agents through the hallway toward the lobby.

"Your partner, Thompson's not gonna be happy about this," whispered Cassi.

"Don't worry about him," Wilkes said, quietly. "Your Captain and I made a call to my superiors and they jumped at he chance to bring you in on this when they read a copy of your file and some of the reports you wrote concerning this case. It's out of Thompson's hands now." Cassi nodded and they continued to follow their team through the lobby and onto the parking lot, where the vans were parked.

The infiltration had gone well. With false credentials, Cassi posed as potential secretary seeking employment at the Techno Computer Company and was hired almost immediately. The first three weeks of her employment were uneventful. Then one evening she was filing some documents and one of the papers slipped out of its folder. Cassi picked up the document and was about to replace it when something got her attention. It was a memorandum containing a list of payoffs from various areas of Los Angeles and some from Santa Bella and Burbank to a man name Steven Corey Polito. Quickly making copies of the document, Cassi replaced the memorandum in the folder than folded the copies and stuffed them into her coat pocket. She checked her watch. It was 4:15 p.m., almost time to go.

She went to the brewer around the corner for some coffee, filled a cup and was on her way back to her cubicle when two young ladies, one blonde the other a brown haired brunette, passed her, engaged in a deep conversation. Curious, Cassi followed them back to the coffee maker and stopped out of their sight, listening from around the corner.

"You really think something happened to her?" said the blonde, as her friend filled her cup.

"It makes sense," replied the brunette. "I mean look at it. Jeanette talks about quitting and starting her own business. Then all of a sudden whoosh, and she's gone."

"Maybe that's what she did," said the blonde. The brunette took a sip of coffee and shook her head. "Angie, I've known her longer than you and she's never been one to act impulsively, plus I went to visit her and her babysitter said she never returned. The cops have been looking for her for weeks."

Angie filled her coffee mug in stunned silence as her friend continued. "And what about William Thompson? He was supposed to be going to Colorado. No one's seen or heard from him since."

"Oh come on, Joanna," said Angie. "That doesn't mean anything. He's moving to an entirely different state. That's hardly any cause for alarm, or suspicion."

"Well, maybe not. But something funny is going on in this company," insisted Joanna.

"If something is going on, I wouldn't let on that I knew," warned Angie. "If the right people overhear, you may be the next to disappear."

"But that's just it. I don't know what's going on."

"They're not going to know that," said Angie.

Cassi finished her coffee and checked her watch again, 4:25 p.m. She went back to her desk, got her time card, and joined the other workers at the clock.

Later in the van, Cassi reviewed her findings with the team. She passed out copies of the memorandum she found.

"Good Job, detective. This may be just what we need," said Wilkes, scanning the document.

"But does the name Steven Corey Polito ring a bell with any of you?" asked Cassi. The federal operatives looked the copies over and concentrated, but none of them could come up with anything. Even Wilkes was baffled, and he'd studied the document harder than anyone. He finally said, "No, no one I can remember." The other agents shook their heads as well.

Cassi laid her copy of the document on a console and motioned for the agents to gather around.

"Here we have the name Steven Corey Polito, but if we take a few letters from each name, look at what we get." Cassi wrote the name down and dissected it. Steven [S] Corey [Cor] Polito [Pio}

"My God," gasped Tawny. "She's right.

"There it is in black and white," said Wilkes, stroking his chin.

"Of course that may not mean much, but it's hunch I'm willing to play, wouldn't hurt to put his name in the computer and run a make on him."

Wilkes looked at Cassi. "No wonder your captain has such faith in you."

"There's something else," said Cassi. "I caught some cross talk from a couple of girl's concerning a couple of disappearance from the company."

"Yeah, we got every word they said," said Tawny, lightly patting the tape recorder on one of the consoles.

"I'll radio headquarters in the morning and get some reinforcements to investigate the agencies on this list," Wilkes said. "Again, good work, lieutenant."

"Thanks, just doing my job," said Cassi. But she had a suspicion about the memorandum she'd found. Why would Scorpio keep it where someone could easily find it? A document such as that should have been locked up and secured, unless it was *meant* to be found. Cassi couldn't be sure, but she was going to keep her eyes open.

CHAPTER 16
CASE CLOSED

Scorpio was furious. During the last few weeks his investments had been hit hard by elements of the FBI and the DEA (Drug Enforcement Agency). Huge shipments of heroin and cocaine, as well as several arsenals he owned had been confiscated and his men either captured or killed. Only Nick Freeman and a handful of other lieutenants managed to evade the huge dragnet that blanketed both Santa Bella and Los Angeles. And though Scorpio knew who was behind the raids, his men had come no closer to catching the elusive young detective, which made the situation even more frustrating.

    He'd wanted to kill her himself, slowly and painfully so he could look into her eyes as she died. Then he would cut out her heart, put it in a jar, and display the gruesome trophy in his office for all to see, an unending reminder of his savage triumph. But now, as he sat in his office with what was left of his men, he issued an ultimatum. Pounding his fist on his desk, he yelled, "I want her dead! Do you hear me? No matter what it takes, do it at any cost! And when she's dead, bring her body here to me, now go!"

    The frightened men fell all over themselves not so much as to carry out the orders, but to get away from Scorpio's fearsome presence. All of them that is, except Freeman, who strolled away calmly as ever. As Scorpio's men were passing the secretarial cubicles on the third floor, Freeman glanced to his left and saw a lovely young secretary wearing a white knit top, white leather skirt, and matching thick-heeled pumps putting some folders into a file cabinet. Always considering himself a ladies' man, he started to go flirt with her when something jarred his memory. Her face, the way she stood, her jet-black hair and shapely, athletic build, the way she walked after she left the cabinet. Even through the fake glasses she wore, there was no doubt in Freeman's mind that he was looking at Cassi Day. *Son of a gun!* he thought to himself. He and the others had been trying for weeks to capture her and here she was, right under their noses the whole time. His surprise quickly gave way to anger, as he watched her. The first time they'd tangled was humiliating enough, but now she'd made a fool of him twice.

    Silently he got the other men's attention and motioned them into a semi-circle, speaking to them in low tones.

    Unknown to Freeman and his men, Cassi had seen them looking at her and sensed the danger, which was why she'd closed the cabinet and gone to the restroom. She made sure she was alone, then whispered into her microphone, "Wilkes."

"I'm here," he answered. "Go ahead, detective."

"I got trouble," Cassi said. "A guy I tangled with works here."

"Did he get a good look at you?"

"I think so, he stood there long enough."

Wilkes pondered the situation. He glanced at Tawny, who looked at him questioningly. Before he could speak, Cassi broke the silence. "Stay put. If I'm found out, they'll take me right to Scorpio."

"Still playing those hunches, lieutenant?" asked Wilkes.

"You bet. As much trouble as I've caused him, I'm sure he wants to kill me himself." Cassi said.

"Is the tracer in your belt still secure?"

Cassi hooked her thumb behind her belt buckle and touched the small, magnetic device. "Yeah, I still got it."

"We'll be standing by," said Wilkes.

"Check." She signed off.

The men were gone when Cassi went back to her desk, and she finished her shift without incident. It wasn't until she was clocking out, when she was approached by a dark-haired man in a gray business suit.

"Excuse me, are you the new secretary, Miss Kimberly Thomas?" he said.

"Why yes, I am." Cassi said, a bit apprehensively.

"I'm Ronald Stevens, assistant director of this company." He extended his hand and Cassi shook it. "I hope I didn't alarm you."

"Well, just a bit." Cassi admitted.

"I'm terribly sorry, but what I wanted to say was that we've been watching your progress here with a great deal of interest."

"We?" asked Cassi.

"Yes, the director and myself. And I must say we're quite impressed with you. No one we've hired has ever adapted as quickly and efficiently as you have, and the director himself would like to talk with you about a commendation and a possible promotion. He would've come to see you himself, but he's in a meeting right now."

Cassi was skeptical. She knew Stevens was lying, for she'd only been there a month and had done no more or less work than any of the other secretaries. And she'd never known any secretary to be promoted so quickly. "When does he want to see me?" she said.

"Right now. It won't take long." Stevens said, smiling.

"Okay," said Cassi. She followed him to the elevator, which went down to drop off a few passengers, bound for home. Stevens pressed the up button and the elevator ascended and kept going until it reached the top floor. Cassi felt uneasy. Adrenaline began to course through her and her muscles tightened. She knew something was wrong, but played it off. Her premonition was realized as the elevator doors opened and four men rushed into the elevator and surrounded her.

"Hey, what is this?" she said, as they grabbed her. "What are you doing?"

"Shut up!" barked one of the men as they pulled her off the elevator. They held her, while Freeman walked casually up and stuck the muzzle of his Colt 45 under her chin. "We meet again, Miss Day."

"I don't know who or what you're talking about," Cassi said.

"Really? Well, let's see if I can refresh your memory." And with that, he gave her a backhanded slap across the left temple. The force of the stinging blow snapped her head painfully to one side and sent her glasses flying down the carpeted hallway.

Gritting her teeth against the pain, Cassi glared murderously into Freeman's eyes. "How's your memory now?" asked Freeman.

"Still a little fuzzy," Cassi said, defiantly.

"Get her out of here," growled Freeman. The men took Cassi down the hall and Freeman followed, stepping on and breaking her glasses as he went.

In the van, agent Tawny Campbell pounded her fist on the console. "Jeez! Her cover's blown!" She started to vacate her chair but Wilkes put a hand on her shoulder.

"No not yet," he said.

"What are you talking about? They're going to kill her if we don't get her out!" cried Tawny.

"She knew what she was getting into. Besides we need to get that scumbag's confession on tape, then we can nail him for good." Tawny knew Wilkes was right. They were just minutes away from closing a case that had dragged on for four years, and had come too far to turn back now. She reluctantly sat back at the console, put on her headphones and listened helplessly to Cassi's plight.

Cassi was shoved roughly into a large office with plush navy carpeting and several framed portraits lining its brown paneled walls. To her left was a huge window, covered by heavy, navy curtains, which had been pulled neatly back to expose a beautiful view of the city. In front of the window was a highly polished, oak desk and seated behind it, with his back to her, was Scorpio. The chair swiveled and Scorpio turned to face, for the first time, the young woman who'd virtually destroyed his organization. His icy blue eyes regarded her for a few moments before he spoke.

"Good evening, Miss Day," he said, frigidly.

"So, you're Scorpio. You killed a lot of good people, you butcher!" snarled Cassi, struggling in the grip of the men who held her. Scorpio glanced at the two men holding Cassi and lightly waved his hand. Instantly they released her and backed slowly away, their hands on their guns.

Cassi glanced behind her at the receding men, and then looked back at Scorpio. "You must really think I'm a dangerous woman to be packing that kind of firepower," she said.

"Caution is very important in our business, said Scorpio. "But I would imagine you have several questions, so please feel free to ask."

"Where does a business tycoon like you benefit from murder? That's not going to help your company very much."

"Murder? Really detective, is that the limit of your vision?"

"Enlighten me." Cassi said, folding her arms.

"Well, you're correct. If computers and real estate were all I cared for, life would be without challenges. My real desire, detective, is power. And there are many places here and abroad where I can obtain it. But to obtain certain types of power, one must use a tool, and murder is a tool that I find very effective. Scorpio took a remote control from his desk, pointed it past Cassi, and pressed a button. Instantly the wall behind her slid open to reveal a large screen. Scorpio touched another button and a video recorder played schematics of buildings and corporations.

"Take a look, detective," he said. Microsoft, Apple, IBM, all companies of unlimited power that'll be mine once I've bought them."

"So that's where your drug cartels, gun running, and racketeering come in," said Cassi.

"Very perceptive, Miss Day." Scorpio said.

Cassi turned to face him. "And what makes you think these companies are going to sell out to you?"

"Everything has its price, Miss Day. If they prove stubborn, I'll have to persuade them."

"And how do you plan to do that?"

"By kidnapping their key officials and holding them for ransom."

"You're crazy," hissed Cassi.

"Am I?"

"And I suppose that anyone who knew of your plans and tried to leave this syndicate, came down with a severe case of death, like William Thompson and Jeanette Scott?"

"Like I said, Miss Day, murder is merely a tool. I couldn't allow any information to leak. Thompson and Scott came across some documents they shouldn't have, so of course they were disposed of."

"Boss," said one of his men, approaching. He whispered something to Scorpio and handed him Cassi's purse. She swore under her breath as the syndicate boss opened the purse and pulled out a miniature tape recorder. Scorpio hit the stop button and then looked at Cassi. "Really detective, I would've expected something better from Santa Bella's finest…How pathetic." He removed the tape and unraveled it.

"Wilkes, we've got him!" cried Tawny.

"What?" Wilkes rushed to the console and put on some headphones as Tawny rewound Scorpio's confession. He smiled as he listened. Jerking the headset from his ears, he addressed his team. "Contact the LAPD and gear up. We're going in."

Tawny chambered a round in her pistol. "Hang on, Cassi!"

As his men held Cassi, Scorpio walked toward her and cupped her chin in his hand. "You're a very lovely woman, detective," he said. "It's a shame that I'll have to kill you."

Disgusted, Cassi jerked her chin from his hand and glared into his eyes. She inwardly shivered at what she saw in those two frigid pools of pale, blue ice. She saw a man with no heart, conscious, or soul, who'd killed countless people without pity or remorse, and would soon add her to his list. Scorpio looked at Freeman and said, "Take her to my yacht and wait for me there." Freeman nodded and motioned with his pistol for the other men to bring Cassi along.

The late evening sun cast long shadows on the sidewalks and parking lots of the Techno Computer facility as Scorpio's men dragged Cassi Day's struggling form out of the building. A black limousine drove around to where they were and its door opened to receive its unwilling passenger.

"Let go of me!" Cassi ordered, through clenched teeth, as she struggled violently against the men trying to force her into the dark vehicle. Freeman walked up and again and put his gun muzzle under her chin. "You make one more move, and I'll finish you right here!" He said, icily.

"Hey man, come on. Let's go!" said someone inside the car. Freeman took his eyes off her to see who'd spoken and Cassi kicked the pistol out of his hand. She then kicked him full in the chest, knocking him backward away from her. While the men holding her were still off guard, Cassi wrenched her right arm free and elbowed her captor in the sternum, doubling him over. She then chopped him at the base of his skull, knocking him senseless to the ground. Turning quickly, Cassi felled the man holding her left arm with a hard right cross to the temple.

Freeman was trying to crawl to his fallen gun, but Cassi rushed over and stomped on his wrist just as his hand grasped the gun handle. Howling in agony, he jerked his hand from under her foot, and she kicked the weapon just out of his reach. As Cassi squatted to collect the weapon, an object touched her back and before she could react, a button was pressed and volts of electricity surged painfully through her body. She screamed and fell to the pavement. As she looked dizzily upward, she saw a man standing over her with a tazer in his hand.

Summoning her fading strength, Cassi formed her right hand into a knife and chopped upward into the tazer man's groin. In pain the man dropped the weapon and bent over holding his crotch, but Cassi didn't stop. Her left fist shot up and connected solidly with his chin, knocking him backward onto the hood of the limousine.

Freeman had retrieved his weapon and was taking aim at Cassi, who'd climbed to her feet and was viciously punching the man who'd shocked her. A shot sounded and Cassi turned to see the ex marine clutch his bloody chest and fall to the ground, never to rise again. Cassi looked around to see Wilkes holding a smoking 45 in his hand, as Tawny and the other agents rushed in and captured the other syndicate men.

"You all right?" said Wilkes.

"Yeah," answered Cassi, panting. "But we don't have much time. Scorpio's going to his yacht."

"How do we get there?"

Cassi looked at the beaten syndicate men and said, "One of these jerks will know." Grabbing the closest of the prisoners, she growled, "How do we get to Scorpio's yacht? You've got five seconds to tell me before I snap your neck like a dry twig!"

The frightened man looked into her smoldering eyes and stammered "A chopper's gonna meet him on t-the roof."

Cassi let go of the man and picked up Freeman's gun, which had a full magazine. She looked up at the towering building then, without a word, dashed back into the complex.

"Wait!" called Wilkes, running after her, but too late, Cassi boarded an elevator and was gone.

Scorpio stood alone on the roof as he waited for his private helicopter to pick him up. He felt good. Cassi Day, a constant thorn in his side, had been captured and was soon to be disposed of. He stood there, smiling grimly to himself, anticipating the look in her eyes as she drew her final breath, slowly dying by his murderous hands. From the distance came the *Whup! Whup! Whup!* of chopper blades and the syndicate boss looked up to see a tiny spec in the blue sky coming slowly but steadily toward the complex. Within minutes, Scorpio's victory would be complete.

Aboard the ascending elevator, Cassi's patience grew shorter, as the elevator seemed to take forever. She checked the weapon, making sure the safety was off. At one point she even pounded the side of her fist against the wall. "Come on, you bucket of bolts!" she growled, through her teeth. " The seasons move faster!" The elevator stopped on the 70th floor and Cassi flipped the red switch on the control console and charged down the hallway to

Scorpio's office. Chambering a round in her pistol, she took a deep breath and kicked the door in. The office was empty as she'd suspected, but she felt she had to take the gamble.

She'd just stepped out of the office, when something heavy cut through the air, heading for her head. Cassi ducked just as a foot swung over her head and kicked the doorpost where she'd stood. She straightened to face one of the syndicate men and saw two others charging up the hallway toward them. The first attacker punched at her, but Cassi sidestepped the blow, grabbed his arm and flipped him over her shoulder. She clubbed him across the head with her pistol, knocking him cold, as the other men closed the gap. Cassi uncoiled a fierce back kick, which hit the nearest man in the stomach. She then gave him a hard back fist strike to the temple, which sent him staggering backward into his partner, who shoved him aside and aimed his pistol at her. The young officer dodged out of the way just before the pistol fired. She took cover in Scorpio's office and returned fire, as the syndicate man ducked into a doorway down the hall from her, still shooting.

I don't have time for this, Cassi thought to herself, as the bullets zipped past her and cracked into the wall outside the door. She looked down and saw a pistol sticking out of the waistband of the first man she'd decked. Taking a deep breath, she somersaulted into the hallway, snatched the pistol from the unconscious form, and thumbed the safety off. She jumped to her feet and charged down the hall toward her attacker, yelling at the top of her lungs and with both pistols blazing. The man leaned out the door and fired again, but his weapon clicked empty. Still running, Cassi leaped into the air and delivered a flying sidekick to the man's chin, which snapped his head back and broke his neck. He fell to the floor in a heap.

Cassi heard chopper blades approaching and knew there was no time to lose. She hurriedly vacated the office and searched frantically through the hall for a stairwell leading to the roof, finding one, she rushed up the stairs only to find the door to the roof was locked. The helicopter was almost on top of the building as Cassi rammed her shoulder against the frozen door, but to no avail it wouldn't budge. Desperately, she aimed her weapon at the latch and fired twice. The door sparked as her bullets tore through the latch and the acrid smell of cordite stung her nostrils as the young detective took a step back, concentrated, and burst the door open with a well-aimed kick.

The chopper had landed neatly on the roof and Scorpio was about to climb aboard when one of his men leaned outward and sprayed the roof with machine gun bullets. The syndicate boss looked back in time to see Cassi take cover behind a cooling unit. He smiled at her persistence. She was truly a worthy adversary. Looking back at his men, he said, "Leave me."

"What?" said the pilot.

"Come back for me in ten minutes."

The door gunner started to protest, but a warning look from Scorpio changed his mind. Scorpio then removed his sport jacket, tie, and shirt then he took off his shoes and socks. Clad only in a black tank top and gray slacks, the syndicate leader stood alone as the helicopter rose into the air. Cassi Day, weapon ready, peered over the cooling unit and watched as the helicopter ascended and soared away.

"Come, miss Day!" called Scorpio, walking forward. "You came all the way from Santa Bella to fight me. Now's your chance."

Cassi walked slowly from behind the cooling unit, her weapon trained on Scorpio. "I'm right here, Scorpio!"

"I hear you're very good with your hands and feet," said Scorpio.

"Good enough," said Cassi.

"Well, are you going to hide behind a gun or face me one on one?"

Cassi took a deep breath and slowly lowered her weapon. After a few moments she flung the pistol aside completely.

"I knew you couldn't resist my challenge." Scorpio said.

Cassi walked slowly toward the lean, muscular figure standing before her. "I'm taking you in, Scorpio. We can do this easy or hard." *And I hope you want it hard*, she thought. Scorpio smiled and moved into an offensive position as Cassi removed her shoes and took a defensive stance.

A light, cool breeze blew across the roof as the two enemies faced and sized each other up. For a long moment neither of them moved then Scorpio attacked with a back fist strike, which Cassi deflected downward and then came up her own back fist strike, which hit the syndicate boss squarely in the eye. As he reeled from her blow, Cassi jumped into the air and did a spinning crescent kick, but Scorpio ducked. He heard her foot whoosh over his head with enough force to have killed him had it hit him.

Scorpio took advantage of her vulnerability and delivered a swift palm strike, which caught Cassi in the stomach, knocking the wind out of her. As she doubled over, Scorpio laced his fingers together and bashed her across the back of her head, knocking her to her knees. He kicked her in the ribs as she tried to get to her feet.

The young detective rolled with the force of the kick and came up on her hands and knees, as Scorpio stalked her. When he was close enough, she executed a foot sweep that knocked his legs from under him. The syndicate boss fell painfully onto his back, but was up in a second using a catapult move while Cassi climbed shakily to her feet, wincing at the pain in her side.

"So, you're not all talk after all," chided Scorpio. "I love a spirited game!"

"*Kiiiyaa!*" screamed Cassi, as she executed a fierce lunge punch, which her nemesis easily deflected and responded to with an amazingly fast roundhouse kick. But Cassi's reflexes were even quicker. Flinging up both hands, she parried the kick, simultaneously trapping his leg. Scorpio gritted his teeth in pain as Cassi fired her elbow downward into his knee joint. "You didn't need that leg, did you?" she taunted.

Having turned the syndicate men over to the police, Wilkes and his team were on their way up on one the two lobby elevators. Some of the team members were anxious for more action, but Wilkes and Tawny's thoughts were with Cassi. "I can't believe she just took off like that," said Wilkes. "God only knows how many syndicate members we're running into and she's gone to fight them all."

"She's either the most courageous woman I've ever seen, or she's the craziest," said Tawny.

"I prefer to think the former and not the latter," said Wilkes.

"Me too," Tawny said, quietly. The elevator stopped on the 70th floor and the federal agents rushed up the hallway and checked the still forms of the syndicate men.

"Two of 'them are still breathing," said Weathers.

"Take them into custody." Wilkes said, looking around for Cassi. The sprawled bodies lying all over the hallway indicated that she'd been there, but where was she now? There had to be some way to get to the roof. Just then, Tawny located the stairwell and called to Wilkes, who motioned for his team to follow him.

Scorpio pummeled Cassi with lefts and rights, slowly driving her toward the edge of the building. The last blow hit her in the temple and she fell on her back. Hearing his chopper returning, Scorpio looked down at the young woman sprawled at his feet. "You've been a worthy opponent, Miss Day," he said. "But I'm afraid I must take my leave. Give my regards to your partner." He knelt down and began to strangle her.

Cassi pulled desperately at his hands as they tightened around her throat, but they were too strong. She felt him drag her steadily toward the roof's edge and her strength was fading from lack of oxygen. She'd fought hard and had made a courageous effort, but it looked as if Scorpio was going to win, as her strength steadily faded.

Across the roof Wilkes and his team came through the broken door, looking around frantically for Cassi. It was Tawny who saw Scorpio kneeling over the young detective's nearly inert form at the edge of the roof. "Oh God! We're too late!" she gasped.

"Scorpio!" yelled Wilkes, aiming his pistol. But before the federal operative could shoot, Scorpio's chopper swooped down on a strafing run and sprayed the roof with bullets. Some of the agents managed to take cover in time, but some were cut down by the murderous machine gun. The enemy chopper passed over and then doubled back for another attack.

Cassi lay in total darkness, Scorpio's fingers steadily tightening on her throat. Her strength was nearly gone and she knew that death was reaching out for her, eager to embrace her and carry her away. As the last of her strength faded, a light cut through the black fog and she saw Mickey's smiling face for a fleeting moment, then the joyous image was replaced by another image, his inert body lying in the hospital, surrounded by nurses. She then heard captain Warden's voice. "How do you think you'll honor Mickey if you get yourself killed out there?"

Suddenly filled with new strength, born from hatred, Cassi's eyes popped open and a white-hot rage exploded through her. She reached up and gripped his throat, driving her thumb into the hollow area above the clavicle. Keeping one hand on his throat, Cassi's other hand slid down and gripped his genitals. Sitting halfway up, the young officer suddenly rolled backward and flipped the syndicate leader off her.

As Scorpio lay on his side, coughing and holding his groin, Cassi leaped to her feet and attacked. She tried to kick him in the head, but the resilient boss dodged her attack and grabbed her foot. Climbing quickly to his feet, he slung her foot away from him in a circular arc. Cassi spun around with the momentum and chopped him across the throat. Screaming like a woman possessed, Cassi fired lefts and rights into his face and body, beating him into a stupor. She grabbed his shoulders and fired her knee into his sternum.

"That's for Mickey!" she snarled. She then gave him a hard uppercut to the chin. "That's for Tina!" Filled with hate and adrenaline, Cassi jumped into the air and did a spinning heel kick, which hit Scorpio solidly in the face, knocking him off the roof. Cassi looked over the edge as the syndicate boss fell screaming toward the pavement below. "And that was for me!" she hissed.

Hearing shots behind her, Cassi whirled around to see the FBI agents locked in a shootout with the men in Scorpio's chopper. She glanced hurriedly around for her pistol and saw it lying a few yards from the cooling unit. The helicopter came right at her, the door gunner aiming his weapon. Cassi ran forward and dove into a front handspring, landing with her hands on the weapon as submachine gun bullets ripped into the roof all around her. Cassi somersaulted to her feet, as the syndicate chopper passed over her. She spun around and fired at the receding chopper. Two of her bullets hit the door gunman and one shell whacked into the fuel tank.

Cassi fell on her stomach and covered her head as the helicopter exploded into a thousand fiery pieces, which rained onto the helipad. Cassi Day climbed to her feet and stared at the flaming wreckage. "Your flight's been canceled," she said, darkly.

Behind her, Wilkes and the surviving members of his team stared in awed silence at the battered and bruised detective. "I'm glad she's on our side," Wilkes whispered.

"You got that right." Tawny said, quietly.

Weeks later, Cassi awoke from troubled sleep. Bathed in sweat, she pulled back the covers, got out of bed, and went to the kitchen for a glass of orange juice. The events of the past month had left her physically and mentally drained. She'd picked Tina up and had seen her safely to the airport and after a tearful farewell, returned to a hero's welcome at the police station and to what seemed like sixteen tons of paperwork, which had snowed her over. But the biggest joke had been FBI agent Thompson, who'd tried to file charges against her for obstructing justice. But agents Tawny Campbell and Wilkes had vouched for her as well as the chief agent in charge of the case, and Cassi had told Thompson, not too politely, where he could go and walked out of the office.

It was all behind her now. The case was closed and Mickey's killers had been dealt with. Cassi walked over and sat on her couch, drinking her juice and trying to clear her mind. She was exhausted. Captain Warden had graciously given her some vacation time, but she'd found it hard to relax. She turned on her TV and watched it until she finally dozed off at dawn.

Cassi awoke at 12:30 p.m. and put on some blue jeans, sneakers, and a red and white football jersey and left the house, locking the door behind her. She got into her car and drove to the cemetery where Mick was buried. When she found his grave she knelt next to it and said, "You can rest easy now, Mickey. The animals who did this to you are history." Tears ran down her face as she continued, "I'm gonna miss you, partner. I swear I won't forget what you taught me." Cassi stood, brushed away her tears, and headed for her car. When she was halfway there, she stopped and looked back at Mickey's grave. "Goodbye, big brother," she whispered.

When Cassi reached her car, the police radio came to life..."Robbery in progress near Third Street ...all available units respond." Thumbing the talk button, Cassi answered, "Five-oh-six responding." She switched off the radio, started her car, and headed toward the fracas, her blue light flashing on her dashboard. She knew she was supposed to be resting, but as long as there was crime on Santa Bella's streets, Cassi Day couldn't rest. No matter what, she was going to do her part.

THE END.